Henry Lonsdale

The Life of John Heysham, M.D.

And his Correspondence with Mr. Joshua Milne

Henry Lonsdale

The Life of John Heysham, M.D.
And his Correspondence with Mr. Joshua Milne

ISBN/EAN: 9783744734998

Printed in Europe, USA, Canada, Australia, Japan

Cover: Foto ©Raphael Reischuk / pixelio.de

More available books at **www.hansebooks.com**

THE LIFE

OF

JOHN HEYSHAM, M.D.

AND

HIS CORRESPONDENCE WITH MR. JOSHUA MILNE
RELATIVE TO THE CARLISLE BILLS
OF MORTALITY

EDITED BY

HENRY LONSDALE, M.D.

o. є. μ.

LONDON
LONGMANS, GREEN, AND CO.
1870

Neglecta reducit, sparsa colligit, utilia selegit, necessaria ostendit, sic utile.

BAGLIVI.

—— Non, me ut miratur turba, laboro,
Contentus paucis lectoribus.

JOHN GRAUNT.

.

IN GRATEFUL

REMEMBRANCE OF LASTING FRIENDSHIPS

I DEDICATE THIS VOLUME

TO

JAMES ADAMS, M.D., GLASGOW.

ROBERT BROWN, F.R.C.S., CARLISLE.

WILLIAM L. DICKINSON, L.R.C.P., WORKINGTON.

JOHN GRAHAM, M.D., LONDON.

DAVID R. LIETCH, M.D., KESWICK.

ROBERT G. LORD, M.D., H.M.S., INDIA.

THOMAS LOY, M.A. Cantab., STOKESLEY.

WILLIAM A. LOY, M.R.C.S., GREAT AYTON.

GEORGE A. MEIN, M.D., AUSTRALIA.

JOHN NICHOLSON, M.D., HEXHAM.

ANTHONY PEAT, M.R.C.S., WORKINGTON.

ROBERT TIFFEN, M.D., WIGTON.

787

CONTENTS.

CHAPTER VI.

CHAPTER VII.

CHAPTER I.

THE name and family of Heysham are of ancient date and record in the county of Lancaster. The district bordering on Morecambe Bay, now constituting the manor and parish of Heysham, was at an early period taken possession of by a roving Saxon chieftain named Hessa, from whose occupation of it the name is derived. After the Norman Conquest it appears as "*Hessam*," part of the possessions which Earl Tosti had held, and was then granted by the Conqueror to some one of his followers, who, according to the fashion of those times, assumed the name "*de Hessam.*" In the reign of Henry III. it was in the holding of Roger de Hesham, by the tenure of serjeanty, or service of *Cornage ;* which was to be in attendance on the border of the county with horn and white wand whensoever the King should come, to introduce him with sound of horn into the county, and in like

B

manner to attend him on his departure. From this conspicuous service of *cornage* it is traditionally said that the Lords of the Manor of Heysham acquired the surname of *Cornet*, eventually transformed into *Gernet*, in which name the manor long remained vested. Yet junior branches of the family retained the ancient name ; and in the town of Lancaster there were in the seventeenth century more than one branch bearing it. Thus we are enabled to trace the descent of John Heysham, whose life is to occupy these pages, from a citizen of Lancaster, who flourished there in the early part of that century. This gentleman had two sons, Gyles Heysham and John Heysham. They were merchants and shipowners. Gyles had several children, amongst whom were Robert and William, who both went to London in their youth, and became eminent merchants there ; so much so, that Robert, being an alderman of London and president of Christ's Hospital, was in 1698 elected member of Parliament for his native town Lancaster, and sat as such till 1715, when he was elected for the City of London, and held that position till his death in 1722. William also, in 1705, became representative in Parliament of his native town, and enjoyed the honour as long as he lived. He left by will an estate at Greaves, near Lancaster (now of the yearly value of £200 or thereabouts), for the maintenance of eight poor freemen of the borough.

The second son, John, had also several children—no less than nine of whom were sons. Some of these, following the commercial instinct of the family, emigrated to America, and there realised fortune and position. One son, Gyles, maintained the family name at home. As a shipowner, he shared in the prosperity that attended Lancaster in her extensive sugar trade and other commercial relations. He has been described as handsome in person, and a thorough-bred man of business ; yet, like other men of bold enterprise, he was not uniformly successful in his commercial undertakings. About the year 1750 he took to wife Anne Cumming, daughter of a well-to-do yeoman or " Statesman," at Holme, in Westmoreland, of which marriage came John Heysham, the subject of the present memoir, born at Lancaster on the 22d November 1753.

John Heysham seems to have inherited a good deal of his father's handsome personality and habits of perseverance, and not a little of his mother's thrift ; and both qualifications were serviceable in the path he selected for himself in the world. Young Heysham had the benefit of a good classical and general education at the hands of the Messrs. Jenkinson, members of the " Society of Friends," and schoolmasters of considerable repute at Yealand, a small village near to Burton in Westmoreland. It is worthy of remark that the Quakers were the best schoolmasters of that period in the north of England ; for whilst they inculcated self-denial, industry, and order, they were not less vigilant in training the intellectual powers of their pupils. They unquestionably enjoyed a large share of confidence among the upper middle class. Along Morecambe Bay and the coast further north, in the dales of Westmoreland and Cumberland, wherever George Fox's teaching took root, some worthy disciples of the " Friends"* located themselves as schoolmasters, and did infinite service to the cause of education in these northern counties.

On the completion of his schooling, John Heysham was apprenticed for five years to Mr. Parkinson, a surgeon at Burton. There he had to undergo the usual drudgery of a village medical apprentice, under a master who rigidly exacted the performance of every duty, from the mixing of pills and potions even to the rubbing down of " master's horse." " The doctor's lad"—the term applied to a surgeon's apprentice—had to rise early, and often to sit late, to wait his master's return from distant professional visits. The indentures set forth that he was to learn the " art and mystery" of an apothecary, or the preparation and compounding of drugs ; this included the collecting of plants, the making of decoctions, and all the paraphernalia from the working up of crude materials to the neatly-labelled draught for the

---

* John Dalton, the great chemist, and his brother, at Kendal ; the Fletchers of Broughton and Brigham, near Cockermouth, in the last century ; Joseph Saul of Greenrow, Holm Cultram, in Cumberland, are cited off-hand as prominent instances supporting the views expressed above.

rector's spouse or the squire's daughter. Then bleeding, and tooth-drawing, and cupping, came under the art and mystery of surgery. The lad was also expected to keep up his classics, to make his initiative in anatomy and the elements of chemistry, and to have some notions of disease, so as to be able to act in cases of surgical emergency. The system was well calculated to sharpen a lad's wits, and to fit him to rough the world, and a rougher world than country practice was nowhere to be found in his Majesty's dominions ; but it was hardly consistent with the acquirement of a learned profession or the dignity of manners that should embellish the Healing Art. Attending to the stable one hour, and to aloes and rhubarb the next, savoured more of Veterinary than of Human Medicine. An endless round of menial as well as medical duties prevailed in these village surgeries, which the first three decades of the eighteenth century did not entirely sweep away.* To-day all things are changed, and young Esculapius now dashes along the road in smart

---

* The apprenticeship system, with all its faults, had some redeeming virtues : it trained lads up to the work of their lives, it familiarised them with the professional *adjuvantia*, as well as the forms of physiognomical indications of disease. Till very lately, the great majority of English medical practitioners were so educated, and it may be safely advanced that they have shown no inferiority in skill and discriminative judgment to the generation that has sprung up from the modern system of cramming and forced growth. Upon the roll of medical worthies are to be found a host of provincial men, from the days of Jenner, who have promoted the interests of medicine and surgery quite as much as the favoured metropolitan leaders.

clothes, with light cane and kid gloves, deeming himself a suitor for the comeliest of company, even of the lavender sort.

At an early age John Heysham gave indications of a penchant for Natural History. His love of birds was specially manifested, and with the smattering of human anatomy derived in the surgery of his master, his interest for Ornithology became much enlarged. Like all country-educated lads, Heysham coveted field sports ; but as firearms were very cautiously placed in the hands of apprentices, he was in some measure driven to the practice of the bow and arrow in the pursuit of his favourite study of birds. In the present day such a mode will appear puerile to a degree ; it was not so 110 years ago ; nor was the practice of the bow and arrow one whit less successful in aim than the flint and steel musket known as " Old Brown Bess " to English soldiers.

Being furthest removed from the pulsation of new thoughts, the " North Countrie " held long by the customs of the Tudors, be it the wild weapons of war or the enjoyment of the pastimes of peace. Archery might well linger among the descendants of those* whose prowess had been so highly extolled on Flodden Field—

> " With him (Lord Dacres) the bows of Kendal stout,
>   With milke-white coats and crosses red.
>
>   .   .   .
>
> " These are the bows of Kendal bold,
>   Who fierce will fight, and never flee."

---

* In the Border wars (1584) Cumberland and Westmoreland furnished 8350 men. The 300 Kendal men on Flodden Field proved "*hardy men* that went *noo*

Two centuries, it is true, had passed over since these days of chivalry ; but the remembrance of the glory of the past had not been effaced from the north-country dalesman : nay, the practice of archery had come down from sire to son to the Georgian era. Heysham, touched by the rivalry, the more intense that it was bucolic, prevailing among youths of his own age, became an adept at the ancient mode of shooting.

Heysham was far from being an idle apprentice ; for, in addition to his gallipot work, and the minor practice of physic and surgery, he studied classics and mathematics under the Rev. Dr. Hutton, vicar of Burton. In the course of time he finished his pupilage, and prepared for Edinburgh, a medical school of high repute, where he might finish his studies and become a licensed practitioner. He had seen enough of country practice to condemn it *in toto*, independently of its fearful drudgery. The regular practitioner had not the social status due to his professional rank, and much less of the confidence of the public than the itinerant quack. At all times he had to compete with the village black-smith, the barber, and the herbalist, whose " culling of simples "

foote back." They were evidently of the same stamp as the archers of Sir Thomas Curwen of Workington, that were gathered from West Cumberland and by the mountain districts southwards as far as Furness in Lancashire. Both the men and their chief obtained special praise from " Old Bluff Harry," when visiting these parts of his kingdom, and making a clean sweep of the Monastic Abbeys ; *ex. gr.* Furness and others in the North.

under lunar and saturnine auspices impressed the vulgar mind
with uncommon faith. The only chance left the medical man of
counteracting the prevailing quackery, was to prove, and oft to
repeat the proof of, his professional skill and sagacity. Even this
failed to carry conviction against the prejudice and ignorance
besetting other walks than the strictly bucolic life.

To travel from Lancaster to Edinburgh—170 miles—was no
easy matter in Heysham's day. There were no coaches or public
conveyances—posting being usurped by the grandees of the
nation, and seldom adopted even by them—so that walking and
riding, like "Hobson's choice," were the only alternatives. In the
very year (1774) that Heysham left home for the northern
university, the proprietors of the Edinburgh "Fly" announced to
the public, what was received as a startling fact, that their new
conveyance would make the journey between the English and
Scottish metropolis "in ten days, God willing." The "God willing" was a most significant clause in the agreement, for such speed
as forty miles a-day with "the Edinburgh Fly," however much
wished for, was seldom obtained. Moreover, this stage-coach,
"the Fly," came by York over Stainmore, and then proceeded by
Carlisle to Glasgow, and consequently was of no service to
travellers from Lancaster. Some years elapsed before the Mail
was put on the Shap or Kendal road, namely in 1786. Heysham
had to undertake his journey on horseback, a mode of travelling

which, amongst some drawbacks, in a pluviose district especially, had at least the advantage of giving the traveller time to survey the country through which he passed. With his love for natural history and mountain scenery, the journey could not fail to be exciting and agreeable; as each hour revealed a varying landscape of hill and dale, so each stage or resting-place showed its quaint hostelry and quainter folk. Special mention is made of his travel to Edinburgh, as it exercised a marked influence on his future plans ; moreover, in starting from home he meant to find other quarters, so that he came to look at each town and district with the discrimination of a man in search of a new settlement.

His route lay along the old Roman road, and his halting-places for the night were frequently the *loci in quo* of the camps or stations by which the Northern Borders were held in subjection by the Roman legions. Thus he rode from Lancaster (*Longovicum*) to Kendal (*Concangium*), then to Penrith, and so on to Carlisle (*Luguvallium*). He met with little else on the roads than gangs of pack-horses transferring the merchandise of Kendal to the rest of England, no less than 354 horses being employed in the work. The "Kendal green " and " cottons " had lost part of their reputation in 1770; but knit-yarn and worsted stockings engrossed a vast district around, so that Heysham in his journeying would see here and there, in the hamlets by the fell-sides, and in the valleys—

" The spinsters and the knitters in the sun."

The population of Kendal was equal to Carlisle, and its
commercial spirit somewhat higher than the Border City.
Camden had characterised the town " *lanificii gloria et industria
precellens*," and the arms of the Corporation bore " *Pannus
mihi panis ;*" yet Heysham could not be tempted to fix his tent
under the " three teasels of wool-hooks," however rich they might
be in yield of *panis*—the staff of life.

Having crossed the high and barren moorlands of Shap Fells,
and reached Hackthorpe, he came in view of the rich and
expansive valley of the Eden, and the best features of the
Crossfell range of hills, then, descending by the sylvan streams
of Lowther and Eamont, he halted at Penrith.   Though snugly
ensconced under its own Beacon-hill, and in contiguity to the
Lake district, and the fine mountains of Saddleback and Helvellyn,
this spirited little town did not altogether meet his wishes.   Pro-
ceeding northwards, and surveying the Vale of the Peterill from
the heights of Barrock-fell, or still better from Carlton Hill,
having the richly-planted Woodside on his left, and the noted
Corby Woods on his right, he got his first glimpse of Carlisle.
On reaching Harraby Hill,* an eminence but one mile distant, he
obtained the best view of the city, its surrounding walls, the

* Harraby Hill is the *Harrabee* of Sir W. Scott's " Waverley," and locally
known as " Gallows Hill," where so many Scotch rebels, the followers of " The
Pretender," were hanged for high treason.   The heads of the chiefs were spiked
on the Scottish gates, with their faces pointed to their native land.

towering citadel, the donjon-keep of its castle, and the stately cathedral. Situated at the confluence of three rivers, and surrounded by a plain of richly-green meadows, traversed by the smaller streams of the Cauda and Peterill, the broader vale of the Eden being bounded by gradually rising uplands terminating in the Scottish hills and East Cumberland " Fells," Carlisle charmed Heysham at first sight, and that charm continued through life. He knew nothing of the inhabitants of the place, and therefore had no local tie to bias his judgment; it was the walled city robbed of its mediæval and warlike frown by rich pastoral surroundings, and a landscape of awakening interest, that allured his fancy, and eventually decided him to make Carlisle his future home.

Heysham studied physic under Monro, Cullen, Black, and others of fame in Edinburgh, for three years, and obtained his doctor's degree in June 1777. His Thesis *De Rabie Canina* was inscribed to Henry, the son of Professor Cullen, a circumstance indicative of his being on very pleasant terms with the family of the great medical teacher. The subject selected by Heysham for his "Inaugural Dissertation" was by no means a happy one, inasmuch as *rabies canina*, or hydrophobia, on account of its rarity, was unsuited for original inquiry. The writer is informed that Heysham never saw a case in his fifty years' practice. His historical examination of the disease afforded no clue to its elucidation or proximate cause ; hundreds of doctors who have followed in his wake have done no better, and hydrophobia is still a problem in medicine, notwithstanding all the aids brought to bear upon its investigation by a new chemistry, and not less improved pathology and therapeutics.

The thesis displays a great amount of reading, and a thorough acquaintance with the whole subject ; its Latinity, said to have been extolled by his medical teachers, may be judged of by the following quotation, taken at random from the 15th page :— " De symptomatis in cane rabido occurrentibus. Primo canis suum vigorem amittit, minus vividus fit, et, inter obsequium domino præstandum, solitudinem petit. Non latrat, sed murmurat, aliis minitatur ; auribus et cauda demissis, cibum aversatur, et vultus tristitiæ omnia signa exhibet. Postquam hæc symptomata unum, duos, vel tres dies permanserunt, dein canis cito difficulterque respirat ; linguam ore exerit, atque salivam primo parcius movet."*

Immediately after graduating in Edinburgh, Heysham sailed from Leith to Rotterdam, and made a tour through Holland, with a view of improving his medical knowledge under the renowned

---

* Heysham could point to no Arkadian spring, or the Alysson mentioned by Polybius, the water of which was so famed for its cure of the bite of mad dogs as to be the pride of the Kynathians of old ; nor does he in his Thesis note the history of the beautiful Prætides, of the handsome bestowals of their kingly father upon the lucky physician Melampus.

Dutch professors. On his return to England he stayed some time in London, and afterwards visited his family at Lancaster. In 1778 he settled in Carlisle as a physician, bringing with him excellent introductions to the best families in the city. With or without such credentials, however, he would soon have secured friends among the higher educated class, whilst his handsome bearing as a man could not fail to attract the notice of the gentler sex, to whom many a medical man has owed his first and greatest success in practice. He took lodgings in St. Cuthbert's Lane, near the centre of the city; and such was his partiality for this narrow approach to St. Cuthbert's Church, that he afterwards took a house in it, which he continued to inhabit till his death in 1834.

CHAPTER II.

THE "BORDER CITY"—ITS HISTORICAL RELATIONS—ITS ARCHITECTURE
AND SALUBRITY—ITS HYBRID POPULATION—ITS TRADE—THE COR-
PORATION—THE GUILDS—HABITS AND PASTIMES OF THE CITIZENS
ABOUT A HUNDRED YEARS AGO.

CARLISLE, viewed in its Archaic, Roman, Mediæval, and
Modern attitudes, would seem to offer a large and interesting
theme to the historian. Ripe scholarship and various attainments
would be essential to the elucidation of the subject, and difficulties
of no common kind would surround the threshold of the inquiry.
Of the migratory tribes who, tempted by the good fishing and
hunting ground, settled along the banks of the river Eden, and of
their nomad habits, Taranis-worship, and sacrificial rites, there
is but the common conjecture that attributes all the unknown of
the prehistoric era to the Druids of our earthly Pantheon—constituting a kind of British mythology, that of late years has
become highly acceptable to vulgar minds. What is wanted is a
sketch of Carlisle as the seat of the kings of Cumbria; its
relations to the Picts and Scots; its Roman indoctrination; its
Fetishisms, and the graftings thereon of Christianised formulas;

its Witenagemots ; its destruction by the Danes ; its restoration after a two-centuried dilapidation, and the fresh impetus it gained from Norman rule and architecture ; its monastic and baronial subjections ; and its final emergence from these and other crushing influences to constitutional government and civic rights.

Placed between the fires of both sides of the Borders, Carlisle at times hardly knew to whom it owed its allegiance, and notwithstanding the oft-promised blessings of Christian bondship and legitimate rule, it realised neither peace nor repose for centuries. Even with the establishment of the Tudor dynasty, that brought about a more definitive line of action in every department of the realm, a feverish anxiety reigned along the " debateable land " of the Scottish Borders, near to which was Carlisle, a garrisoned town, coveted by both parties in the struggle for supremacy. Queen Elizabeth saw the policy of making Carlisle the residence of the " Lord Warden of the Western Marches," and of strengthening its holdings and defence against the inroads of the Scotch ; and this policy was maintained by her successors on the throne of England for two centuries subsequently.

In Dr. Heysham's day a broad turreted wall encircled the city of Carlisle ; on the south stood the citadel with its frowning barbicans, and on the north the castle was still more prominent, with its battled towers and donjon-keep. The gates of the city— named, in accordance with the direction to which they pointed,

English, Scottish, and Irish—were shut at sunset; and armed
sentinels kept watch and ward over them, as if still threatened
by the Scottish foe. The military parade gave life and colouring
to the otherwise passive character of the city, the denizens of
which were roused from their slumbers by the call of the bugle-
horn, and after the labours of the day were reminded of the
hours of repose by the evening tattoo. To the traveller approach-
ing from the south, as Heysham did a hundred years ago, what
a pleasant picture of the *rus in urbe* type of a city, when "the
sun" shone "fair on Carlisle wa';" and that wall had no other
environs than the meadowed plain, the converging mountain
streams, and the knolled and wooded eminences beyond! With
increasing population the character of the city became changed.
Devoid of archæological thought as well as architectural taste,
persons, guided only by prospective pecuniary advantages, erected
a lot of wretched buildings in close proximity to the gates, and
thus marred not only the beauty of the Border City, but its well-
known natural salubrity.

Another generation had sprung up in Carlisle since the ill-
fated '45, and a feeling of security was being restored along the
Borders. The banner of St. George, floating over the highest
tower of the castle, implied civic fealty to the Hanoverian cause.
Whilst, however, hundreds of middle-aged persons could recount
with freshness of narrative the march of " Bonnie Prince Charlie "

into the city with his kilted clans, and dwell on his chivalrous bearing and smiling courtesies, sympathy for the fallen house of the Stuarts still lingered by other hearths than the strictly Jacobite residents of the Border City.

A rude and quaint form of domestic architecture prevailed in Carlisle a hundred years ago. Houses with gabled fronts bounded the great thoroughfares ; their doorways, central or lateral, porched or projecting, were occasionally adorned with a kind of Gothic arch ; the windows were few and diminutive, and quite as irregular as other parts of the tenement. The chief objects aimed at in building were warmth and security, and, above all other considerations, evasion of the odious window-tax. The doors of dwellings consisted of thick slabs of oak clumsily attached to cross oaken bars, and over their surface a series of projecting knobs in imitation of the iron rivets and studs on the gates of a mediæval fortress. Occasionally the carpenter indulged his fancy by arranging these wooden pins in geometric or grotesque figures. The same style of workmanship is still to be seen in retired country districts in the North of England.

  The Town or Moot Hall occupied a central position ; and near to it were the butcher's shambles and fish-shops. An open well, much frequented by the inhabitants, was under the same roof, and liable to receive part of the liquid waste percolating the subsoil from both these nuisances in the market-place. The

streets were kept tolerably wide, and garden-plots and open
spaces were to be found in various parts of the city.   On the
other hand, narrow confined lanes, wanting both light and air,
were vastly too numerous along the north-eastern wall.   Irregular buildings and deficient sanitary arrangements ruled every-
where ; the city had no public lights, so each citizen had to carry
his own lantern on moonless nights.   Hard or drinking water
was got from draw-wells in the open streets, or from pumps in
dirty lanes ; soft water was brought from the river Eden by
water-carriers, and sold at so much a pailful.   The days of skin-
washing and clean linen had scarcely dawned upon the Carlisle
lieges, content with a summer's bath in the adjacent rivers, or an
occasional dip in the Solway tide, five miles distant.

The folk of Carlisle were not without a large share of
hybridity in their veins.   Upon the aboriginal stem, call it
Kymric or British, or whatsoever you will, had been grafted from
time to time shoots of the noble Roman, of the marauding Saxon,
and hardy Danish sea-rover, till the parent Cumbrian stock had
lost its primordial character in an amalgamation of race elements
almost beyond ethnological distinction.   If the blending of blood
be the right thing for developing a vigorous race, the men of
Carlisle had every chance of reaping its advantages to the full ;
for, introduced to Cumberland from time to time, were people
from the Italian Apennines, the plains of France, the banks of

the Danube, and the coasts of the North Sea. Verily a motley breed ! which it pleases John Bull to designate " Anglo-Saxon "— a term that has done mighty service in penny literature and House of Commons grandiloquence, and now bids fair to find its lowest level at Cockney banquets and Fishmongers' feasts.

It is a matter of regret that Dr. Heysham, in his survey of the population in 1780, showed no interest in the ethnological characters, and took no note of the general *physique* of the people.* Before the Scottish and Irish immigrations to the city became so marked, Carlisle should have offered a chance of investigating the Saxon and Celtic relations of the North Britisher; at any rate, helped to elucidate some of the more salient features of our mixed race. Heysham was content with a simple census, or "counting the noses" of the people, regardless of the Judaic, Celtic, or Roman forms exhibited by his fellow-citizens. Of the 6299 persons living in the city and suburbs of Carlisle in 1780, and the adjacent outlying district that ranked with the urban parishes, Cumbrians and Lowland Scotch in part would constitute nine-tenths. A few Flemish,† and more Irish would make up the remain-

---

* In 1775, Dr. John Hunter, an Edinburgh graduate, made the " Varieties of Man" the subject of his inaugural dissertation. Heysham was then studying in Edinburgh, but does not appear to have been struck with the novelty of Hunter's thesis.

† The establishment of woollen factories in Carlisle in 1753 by a Flemish firm, accounted for the presence of these foreigners in the Border City.

der. With the growing manufactures of the city, the relative proportions became greatly altered; there was a large influx of Irish, chiefly Ulster men, who found their way across the Channel in Whitehaven coal-vessels, and also a considerable accession of industrious Scotch from Dumfriesshire.

This chapter, it should be observed, is introductory to the consideration of the Bills of Mortality, and should embrace the character of the people, their habits, pursuits, and modes of living, and not less the sanitary aspects of the city, so as to facilitate the comprehension of Dr. Heysham's great work—the tabulation of the births, marriages, and deaths, and all that pertained to the health and disease of the Carlisle population.

Speaking broadly, there were only two distinct classes in Carlisle—the industrious poor, and the well-to-do or independent folk. The shopocratic element was much less significant in those days than now; and happily there was not a single mart for the sale of drugs, where poison could be had for the stomachs, and no public print even of the ribald sort to disturb the minds of the un-sophisticated lieges.

In taking the census, Dr. Heysham did not distinguish those engaged in the larger manufactories from those who laboured to supply the trade-wants of the city; or these again from the higher class, who appeared to live for the purpose of having their wants supplied. The producers and consumers were ranked together.

Heysham was a true advocate of the numerical method *per se*, and gave only the smallest possible recognition to the social potencies, such as property, character, and station ; hence he made no distinction between the consumer and the producer.

The export trade of Carlisle consisted of linen, cotton, and woollen goods, bleached and dyed yarns, but chiefly calico-prints : soap, hats, whips, and fish-hooks also had a place in its commercial transactions. None of these trades were particularly injurious to health. The hours of work might be long, and there were no half-holidays to relieve the burthens of the Carlisle operatives. Wages, however, were fairly remunerative for every kind of work, and the agriculture of the district was necessarily promoted with the view of supplying the weekly markets of a thriving population.

The food of the working classes included a fair amount of beef and mutton, vegetables, cheese, milk, and beer. A coarse kind of bread was used of " seconds flour," of wheat with rye and barley-meal, also oatmeal for porridge and scones. Fish was got from the Solway and its tributaries, and sold cheaply : salmon at 1½d. and 2d. a pound ! Dried fish, bacon, and "hung mutton," formed part of the winter supply of animal provisions. The Irish helped to develop the growth of the potato, whilst the Scotch created a demand for oatmeal in the district. Butcher's meat seldom reached 4d. a pound ; potatoes, 1½d. a gallon ; new milk, 1d. or 1½d. a quart ; milk cheese, 2d. a pound ; chickens and ducks, 6d.

each ; and a Christmas goose could be had for 2s.   Flour (wheat)
was about 2s. a stone ; barley, oatmeal, and rye, rather more than
half the price of wheat flour.   Small beer was sold at 2d. a gallon,
and formed a capital beverage ; whilst good home-brewed or
public-house ale only cost 1s. a gallon, each pint of which was served
in flowing measure.   No wonder " John Barleycorn " had his
votaries, when 3d. could obtain two pints of honestly brewed
drink.

On comparing the wages and food prices of that period (1780)
with the present time (1870), the writer is of opinion that the
working men of Carlisle were as well off then as now.   With the
exception of cereals, provisions were only two-fifths or one-half of
the present prices, whilst wages were far from being proportionally
less ; nay, in some instances quite as remunerative, and markedly
superior in one instance, the weaving trade, once the most thriving
occupation in Carlisle.   The notable exceptions to this general
statement are to be found in the wages of masons, joiners, painters,
or the artisans whose services have risen so greatly in value to
meet the growing luxuries of this age.   In reference to wearing
apparel, it ought to be stated, that the majority of people, whether
high or low in station, spun the materials of their own clothing, so
that there was but the preparation and making up of the fabric
for other hands to do.

The drinking habits of a people naturally affect the rate of

mortality. Now of the temperance or intemperance of the period
under discussion, it is not easy to speak with either warranty
or precision. As spirituous liquors were little used, it might be
inferred that the working classes were not so fiery in their cups.
On the other hand, breweries paid handsome profits, and publicans
throve under the auspices of the "Jolly Butcher and foaming
tankard," or "Willie brew'd a peck o' maut." In no age of
English history have the people shown a dislike for good malt.
Beef and beer are recognised features in the national character ;
and as Carlisle was prosperous, and hospitality abundant, there
would be heydays and hours of high jinks promoted by
Bacchanalian fervour. There was some excuse for the circulation
of the jovial cup, considering the few home comforts allotted to the
labouring class, and the total absence of all public entertainments.
If, as often happened, one room had to receive a whole family,
wife and brats, and screaming babies, no wonder the artisan, after
his long day's labour, sought the "Barley Mow," its clean sanded
floor, its cosy fire, and cosier company, where he could have his ale
served in bright pewter by a buxom landlady in smart cap and
ribbons, and radiant in her glow of welcome to thirsty souls and
good customers.

Had the sanitary arrangements of the city and suburbs been
cared for, the bills of mortality, though highly favourable upon the
whole, would have shown a different and a happier result. The

health due to the district was marred by government exactions in the shape of a window-tax, that naturally led the owners of property to shut out the light and air of heaven from the dwellings of the poor, where these life-giving elements were most needed. The narrow lanes and the confined spaces in which many of the industrial classes dwelt, seemed specially contrived to add fuel to the fire that generated fevers, and to spread the seeds of contagion through the city. The Britisher had no thought beyond his food and raiment and home-brewed. Godliness he might assume, but he seemed in profound ignorance of another cardinal virtue— cleanliness. There was also much huddling together of the Irish and Scottish people, in whom too frequently distempers originated or were greatly fostered.

Civic, military, and ecclesiastical powers exercised jurisdiction within the walls. They constituted a triune, but not an unity one and indivisible, like that expressed in the Athanasian dogma. When the co-operation of their authority was most needed, as in the Scottish rebellion in 1745, the civil and military pulled different ways, and so the enemy passed triumphantly within the gates; upon the whole, however, they worked amicably, and held strongly by the coercive method of promoting the cause of order and morals within their jurisdiction.

The Mayor and Corporation were fully endowed with the municipal attributes, so dearly cherished by the provincial mind, and that have come down in all their unsullied characters to an admiring posterity ; they were consequential and fussy to a degree —often meddling, but seldom wisely operative in any direction. The Mayor, oppressed with official dignity, never failed to be stately in order to do credit to the happy accident that raised him from the tallow and treacle cellarage to the highest seat in the city's council ; he would hardly condescend to approach the Moot-Hall stairs without the insignia of the sergeant-at-arms. The gentility of those days (100 years ago) consisted in cocked hats covering powdered wigs—corporate brains, it may be stated parenthetically, belong to the abstract—blue coats, shorts, and hose, and silver-buckled shoes ; but let the reader imagine the Mayor in additional and finer feathers, with white wand held aloft, and supported by tipstaffs in red facings and glaring buttons upon a blue fabric : how emphatically did the *posse comitatus* proclaim to the citizens—" Clear the way for your betters !" If this parade of the pomps and vanities did not suffice for obedience, there were the " Stocks " and " Pillory," in which incorrigibles were exposed on market-days for the edification of bucolic gazers, and the general improvement of the morals of the county.

A puritanic discipline marked the outward rule of the city, but the inner life was probably that of cathedral cities in general, and not of a kind to save either men or women from the ills of the flesh. There were no playhouses, no singing saloons, and no

public diversion for the labouring classes in the city. The last
decade of the century was entered upon before a theatre was
established (1792). The wrestling ring for the display of the
athletic Cumbrian, and so noted now as the arena of our English
Olympian games, was not formed in Carlisle till the race-meeting
of 1809. How was it that under such a *regime* the city obtained
the designation of " Merrie Carlisle ?" Was it a lapsus of speech,
or the irony of a witty historian, laughing in his sleeve at the
Carlisle lieges ; or, if deserved and true, was it from the too free
use of " home-brewed ?"—the only resource of enjoyment to minds
wearied of an unvarying domestic life, and the only reviving
influence to bodies exhausted by daily toil and routine. The
people claimed their cakes and ale as part of their British rights,
and as laudably perhaps as the Corporation would have its
" Jeremiah Wherlings," or other Lowther sycophants ; the military its roystering cornets ; or the Church its dry and dogmatic formalists. The Trade-Guilds* exercised a large social

* The incorporated companies of butchers, merchants, shoemakers, skinners,
smiths, tanners, tailors, and weavers, used to assemble in the Guild Hall of the
city for business and merry-making of the bacchanalian sort. None but those
belonging to the Trade-Guild or Freemen could vote for the city Members of
Parliament, so that when the practice of making " Honorary Freemen " of rich
county proprietors came into vogue, the gentlemen so honoured had to enrol
their names in the books of one of the trade fraternities. Some knights who
had won " military glory" in the battle-fields of Flanders joined the banners of
St. Crispin, and scions of the noble houses of Cumberland and Westmoreland

and still larger political influence in the city and its environs.
They constituted the enfranchised class, and were of course the
most potential agents at the elections for parliamentary represent-
atives of the city; their gala-days were pronounced in character,
and " Ascension Day," with the annual Kingmoor Races, were
the noisiest and merriest of all. It is not improbable that the
joviality of the Guilds, which included both rich and poor, and
placed all parties very much upon an equal footing, gave rise to
the title of " Merrie Carlisle." The writer can ascertain no more
satisfactory explanation of the oft-quoted epithet applied to the
Border City than the history of the Guild saturnalia.

Basking in the sunshine of life and longevity, the Dean of
Carlisle and other dignitaries of the Church, their man-servants
and their maid-servants within the Abbey gates, scarcely, if at all,
affected the bills of mortality. Moreover, the heads of the Cathedral body lent kind aid to Dr. Heysham in all his sanitary
schemes for the benefit of the people. The Church was a great
and respected power in the city ; the commonalty looked with a
kind of awe upon the episcopate in full canonicals and on an exalted
rostrum, preaching doctrines which no man would dare to deny,
even if he felt himself struck on the right cheek by an evangelical
Philistine. This kind of uncharitable conduct could hardly have

were fain to be registered among the tanners and skinners, as if "there was
nothing like leather" in the display of civil privileges.

been met with in the pleasant circle of such divines as Bishop Law
and Dr. Paley; indeed, it is gratifying to add, that the Carlisle episcopate of that day was most ably represented.   Neither talents,
nor amiability, nor the art of good preaching were wanting in its
leading men, who, in classic attainments, in literature, and theology, ranked with the best of England.   Dating from the advent
of Bishop Law in 1767 to the active days of Dean Milner early
in the present century, the Carlisle diocese numbered among its
superior clergy men of high eminence and merit.

CHAPTER III.

THE CARLISLE BILLS OF MORTALITY—TOPOGRAPHY—CLIMATE AND RAIN-
FALL.—CENSUS OF 1763 AND 1780—NOTES ON THE MORTALITY FROM
1779 TO 1787.

DR. HEYSHAM had only been a few months in Carlisle
when he meditated a census of the inhabitants, and the framing
of bills of mortality.   He prefaced his observations on the advantages to be derived from accurate registers of mortality by the
following passages from Percival's *Essays*, vol. ii.—" The establishment of a judicious and accurate register of the births and
burials in every town and parish, would be attended with the
most important advantages, medical, political, and moral.   By
such an institution the increase or decrease of certain diseases,
the comparative healthiness of different situations, climates, and
seasons; the influence of particular trades and manufactures on
longevity; with many other curious circumstances, not more
interesting to physicians than beneficial to mankind, would be
ascertained with tolerable precision.   In a political point of view,
exact registers of human mortality are of still greater consequence, as the number of people and progress of population in

the kingdom, may, in the most easy and unexceptionable manner, be deduced from them. They are the foundation, likewise, of all calculations concerning the value of assurances on lives, reversionary payments, and of every scheme for providing annuities for widows, and persons in old age. In a moral light such *Tables* are of evident utility, as the increase of vice or virtue may be determined by observing the proportion which the diseases arising from luxury, intemperance, and other similar causes, bear to the rest ; and in what particular places distempers of this class are found to be most fatal."

Carlisle, in 54° 53′ N. lat., 2° 55′ W. long., is pleasantly situated on a slightly rising ground, on the south bank of the river Eden, and about five miles above the junction of that river with the tides of the Solway Firth. The Cauda, a mountainous stream, runs within 150 yards of the ancient city on its west side, and the more sluggish Peterill courses about a mile to the south and east ; both streams join the broader Eden, so that Carlisle is placed at the confluence of three rivers, and almost surrounded by them. The tidal Eden is noted for its *Salmonidæ*, and the two tributaries for their special trout-fishing. Along the banks of each river are pleasant walks, from which the Carlisle citizen can obtain commanding views of richly cultivated lands, bounded by elevated mountain-heights, upon which the lights and shadows of a northern sky play with charming fitful beauty.

The subsoil of Carlisle and its immediate vicinity varies a good deal ; sandy or gravelly loam, or these associated with clay, predominate: they rest on the red sandstone. In some of the outlying townships there were tracts of moorish soils, somewhat barren, and in part only enclosed a hundred years ago ; but all this is changed to-day. The meadows around the city are still liable to floods after heavy rains, but there are no stagnant waters and no marshes within or even near the municipal boundary. From the pastoral amphitheatre in which Carlisle is placed, the land rises gradually here and there in undulating line and knolled eminence, but more or less elevating till it assumes a strictly hilly aspect, which culminates about twenty or more miles distant in the mountain ranges of Skiddaw on the south-west, and Crossfell on the east, 3000 feet above the level of the sea. The land-slopes, the river-courses, the varying winds, but chiefly from the south-west, the proximity to the Solway's estuary, and other local conditions, showed favourably for the salubriousness of Carlisle. Dr. Heysham described the air pure and dry. The designation " dry " may seem hardly compatible with the cloudy or pluviose condition of an atmosphere more or less contiguous to the Lake District, proved to be the wettest in England. Dr. Carlyle, the father of the Rev. Mr. Carlyle, the Arabic scholar, kept an account of the quantity of rain which fell at Carlisle during a period of twenty years—namely, from 1757 to 1776

inclusive.* During this period the greatest quantity which fell in one
year was 31.801 inches, the medium being 24.71 inches.   Mr. Pitt
made the mean quantity of rain fallen in Carlisle, from 1801 to
1824, 30.571 inches.   The average rainfall of Carlisle is at present about 28 inches, thus approximating more to Pitt's observations than those of Dr. Carlyle.

Taking the local circumstances into account, Nature had been
lavish in her gifts to the north-western extremity of the vale of
Cumberland, in mountain, wood, and rivers ; here elevations to the
clouds, there a gradual fall to the water's brink.   Man, however,
failed to appreciate the advantages of a site upon which his sons
and daughters might have realised, to the full, the poesy of the
Psalmist and the blessings of health.

* Table of the quantity of Rain which fell at Carlisle during a period of
Twenty years :—

Years.			Inches.	Years.			Inches.
1757	-	-	- 20.026	1768	-	-	- 31.801
1758	-	-	- 26.036	1769	-	-	- 21.803
1759		-	22.946	1770	-	-	- 25.122
1760	-	-	- 28.641	1771	-	-	- 23.982
1761	-	-	- 26.443	1772	-	-	- 28.518
1762	-	-	- 20.538	1773		-	- 28.233
1763	-		- 28.353	1774	-	-	- 19.344
1764	-	-	- 24.162	1775	-	-	- 29.132
1765	-		19.709	1776	-	-	- 21.690
1766	-	-	- 21.472				
1767	-		26.268	TOTAL.		-	494.219

Showing the medium quantity of these twenty years to be 24.71 inches.

In July 1763, at the request of Dr. Littleton, Bishop of Carlisle, the inhabitants were numbered with great care, and the city
and suburbs contained 1059 families, and 4158 inhabitants.

Early in 1779 Dr. Heysham commenced his statistical observations, and set earnestly to work, from week to week and month
to month, to record the births, marriages, the diseases, and deaths,
of the inhabitants of Carlisle. The details and figures given by
Heysham for each year would prove vastly too tedious for all but
the dry-as-dust reader. A brief summary of the more prominent
facts will, it is supposed, best illustrate the character of Heysham's mind, and the nature of his investigations, and, in all
probability, satisfy the requirements of the statist.

It ought to be premised that Carlisle contains two parishes,
St. Mary's and St. Cuthbert's, and that these parishes include the
city, its suburbs, and certain outlying districts, with villages, the
relative population of which divisions is particularly specified in
the following page.

"In January 1780, a very careful and accurate survey was
made by Mr. Stanger and Mr. Howard, under Dr. Heysham's
own inspection, when there were found in the district before
surveyed, 891 houses, 1605 families, and 6299 inhabitants. In
addition to the city and suburbs, the villages contained 257
houses, 267 families, and 1378 inhabitants, as shown in the
accompanying Table No. 1.

TABLE I.

Showing the Population of Carlisle, its Suburbs, and Village District, in 1780.

Parishes of St. Mary and St. Cuthbert's	Houses	Families	Males	Females	Total of both Sexes		Houses	Families	Inhabitants.
English Street	208	319	639	732	1371				
Scotch Street	122	197	354	437	791				
Fisher Street	53	82	130	194	324	Total within the Walls	549	870	3504
Castle Street	81	143	220	307	527				
Abbey and Annetwell Street	77	121	173	270	443				
The Abbey	8	8	17	31	48				
Botchergate	95	202	385	457	842				
Rickergate	82	177	307	356	663	Total without the Walls	342	735	2795
Caldewgate	165	356	592	698	1290				
Newtown	16	19	40	52	92				
Harraby	9	10	31	41	72				
Carleton	30	30	66	67	133				
Wreay	17	18	56	58	114				
Brisco	32	34	107	85	192	Total in the Villages	257	267	1378
Botcherby	21	22	46	52	98				
Upperby	20	21	35	54	89				
Blackhall	63	64	176	178	354				
Cummersdale	22	22	60	50	110				
Morton Head and Newby	27	27	57	67	124				
Total in the two Parishes	1148	1872	3591	4186	7677		1148	1872	7677

Females exceed Males 595. Males to Females as 1 is to 1 and 1-6th nearly.

In Table No. II. he summarised the single and married persons thus :—

TABLE II.

Of the Number of HUSBANDS, WIVES, etc.

	Husbands.	Wives.	Widowers.	Widows.	Total.
Within the Walls . . .	531	569	46	248	1394
Without the Walls . . .	488	522	45	160	1215
In the Villages . .	188	191	17	68	464
	1207	1282	108	476	3073

Total of persons who are or have been married 3073
Total of persons who are married . 2489
Total of persons who never were married . 4604
Total of unmarried persons . 5188
Widows exceed widowers 368
Widowers to widows as 1 is to 4 and 3-7ths nearly.

The astonishing increase of 2141 inhabitants, above half of the original number in the city and suburbs, in the small space of seventeen years (1763-80), Heysham attributed to the establishment of calico-printing manufactories. There were four companies, who daily employed about 800 industrious poor in this kind of work. "This increase of population," Heysham remarked, "had taken place during that very period in which Dr. Price asserts the depopulation of Great Britain to have been rapid and progressive. And what makes this increase more remarkable, Carlisle has, during the whole period alluded to, been constantly supplying the army, the navy, the metropolis, and even the distant regions of India, with her hardy, active, and enterprising sons."

TABLE III.

Of Deaths, Ages, and Conditions.

Ages.	Males	Females	Ages.	Bachelors.	Husbands.	Widowers.	Maids.	Wives.	Widows.	Total.
Under 1 month ..	6	7								
Between 1 & 2 months	2	...	20.30	2	3	...	3	3	1	12
,, 2 & 3 ,,	...	2	30.40	...	3	...	...	3	...	6
,, 3 & 6 ,,	5	...	40.50	...	4	...	2	2	1	9
,, 6 & 9 ,,	2	4	50.60	1	4	2	...	2	1	10
,, 9 & 12 ,,	10	9	60.70	...	11	1	1	4	1	18
,, 1 & 2 years old	21	12	70.80	...	3	3	1	...	7	14
,, 2 & 3 ,,	17	19	80.90	...	1	3	1	1	6	12
,, 3 & 4 ,,	10	8	90.100	...	...	...	1	1	...	2
,, 4 & 5 ,,	6	10	Total of Ages and Conditions	3	29	9	9	16	17	83
,, 5 & 10 ,,	7	7								
,, 10 & 15 ,,	4	3								
,, 15 & 20 ,,	2	2								
Total of the above ages	92	83								

Total of ages under 20 years   { Males   92   Females 83 }   — 175

Total of all ages and conditions 258

From Tables No. III. and No. IV., Heysham "could with pleasure demonstrate the extreme salubrity of Carlisle, even in a very unhealthy year (1779), in which no less than 129 persons were cut off by two epidemic disorders—smallpox and scarlet fever." He proceeded to compare Carlisle with other towns in England as well as on the Continent, and stated that " in Vienna about 1 in 19½ of the inhabitants die annually ; in London,

TABLE IV.

DEATHS and DISEASES of PERSONS of Different Ages.

DISEASES.	Under 5 years.	Between 5 and 10 years.	Between 10 and 15 years.	Between 15 and 20 years.	Between 20 and 30 years.	Between 30 and 40 years.	Between 40 and 50 years.	Between 50 and 60 years.	Between 60 and 70 years.	Between 70 and 80 years.	Between 80 and 90 years.	Between 90 and 100 years.	TOTAL.
FEBRILE DISEASES—													
Inflammatory Fever	3	...	...	...	...	...	...	...	...	...	...	...	3
Nervous Fever	1	...	...	1	...	1	1	...	1	...	...	...	5
Pleurisy	...	...	...	...	...	...	...	1	1	...	...	...	2
Inflammation of the stomach from large dose of steel filings	...	...	...	1	...	...	...	...	...	...	...	...	1
Rheumatism, chronic	...	...	...	...	...	...	...	...	...	1	...	...	1
Gout	...	...	...	...	...	...	...	1	...	1	...	...	2
Smallpox	86	2	1	...	1	...	...	...	...	...	...	...	90
Miliary Fever	...	...	...	...	1	...	...	...	...	...	...	...	1
Scarlet Fever	31	4	2	1	1	...	...	...	...	...	...	...	39
Thrush	2	...	...	...	...	...	...	...	...	...	...	...	2
Consumption	3	2	1	1	5	...	2	3	...	...	...	...	17
Worm Fever	2	4	...	...	...	...	...	...	...	...	...	...	6
NERVOUS DISEASES—													
Palsy	...	...	...	...	...	...	...	1	...	1	...	...	2
Swoon, or Fainting	...	...	...	...	...	...	1	...	...	1	...	...	2
Indigestion	...	...	...	...	...	...	...	1	...	...	...	...	1
Convulsions	2	...	...	...	...	...	...	...	...	...	...	...	2
Epilepsy	...	...	...	...	1	...	...	...	...	...	...	...	1
Asthma	...	...	...	...	...	...	...	1	2	...	...	...	3
Looseness	3	...	...	...	...	...	...	...	...	1	...	...	4
Insanity	...	...	...	...	...	1	...	...	...	...	...	...	1
DISEASES OF THE HABIT—													
Weakness of Infancy	9	...	...	...	...	...	...	...	...	...	...	...	9
Decay of Age	...	...	...	...	...	...	...	...	4	6	11	2	23
Dropsy	...	...	...	...	...	...	1	...	2	...	...	...	3
Dropsy of the head	...	...	1	...	...	...	...	...	...	...	...	...	1
Dropsy of the belly	...	1	...	...	...	1	...	...	...	...	...	...	2
King's Evil	...	1	...	...	...	...	...	...	...	...	...	...	1
LOCAL DISEASES—													
Discharge of blood	...	...	...	...	...	...	1	...	...	...	...	...	1
Costiveness	1	...	...	...	...	...	...	...	...	...	...	...	1
Tumour of the stomach	...	...	...	...	...	...	...	1	...	...	...	...	1
Ulcer	...	...	...	...	...	...	1	...	...	...	...	...	1
Difficult delivery	...	...	...	...	1	1	...	...	...	...	...	...	2
Unknown diseases	6	...	1	...	...	2	2	2	7	3	1	...	24
Accidents	1	...	1	...	2	...	...	...	...	...	...	...	4
TOTAL	150	14	7	4	12	6	9	10	18	14	12	2	258

He classified the diseases under Cullen's *Genera Morborum.*

1 in 20¾; in Edinburgh, 1 in 20⅓; in Leeds, 1 in 21¾; in
Dublin, 1 in 22; in Rome, 1 in 23; in Amsterdam, 1 in 24;
in Breslau, 1 in 25; in Berlin, 1 in 26½; in Northampton and
Shrewsbury, 1 in 26½; in Liverpool, 1 in 27½; in Manchester, 1
in 28; in Chester, 1 in 40; but in the year 1774, when the
smallpox was very general and fatal, 1 in 27; whilst in Carlisle
the mortality was in 1779, 1 in 30⅔."

Heysham looked upon Tables Nos. III. and IV. as "of the
utmost importance to the physician, the politician, and the calculator of annuities; and to every one who has the health and
happiness of himself and family at heart. They clearly demonstrate, as far as one year's observation can have weight, what
periods of life are the most healthy, what are the most obnoxious
to disease.

His tables show that women live longer than men. During
1779, twelve persons died between 80 and 90 years old, eight of
these were females; and the two persons who lived between 90
and 100 years were both females. There were four widows to
one widower, an astonishing disproportion, which he endeavoured
to account for on the following grounds :—1st, Men are in general
more intemperate than women; 2d, They are exposed to greater
hardships and dangers; 3d, Widowers perhaps in general have
greater opportunities of getting wives, than widows have of getting
husbands; 4th, Widows have a greater propensity to live in towns
than widowers; 5th, Women in general, and more especially

among the middle ranks of life, marry earlier than men ; 6th, That as men have " firmer and more robust " constitutions than women, their " muscular and nervous fibres " sooner become stiff and rigid, and less able to meet the " functions necessary to health and life." " But from whatever causes the difference of longevity betwixt males and females may arise, the fact itself is sufficiently ascertained by Table III., where we find that between the ages of 60 and 70, although there are a greater number of wives than husbands, yet eleven husbands and only four wives have died; and of all different ages, 29 husbands and 16 wives."

The mortality from smallpox is worth noting. In the last six months of 1779, 300 persons were seized with smallpox in the natural way, and of these, 90, or nearly 1 in 3, died ! During the same period several hundreds were inoculated in the neighbour-hood of Carlisle, and not one of them died—assuredly a pleasing truth, which led Heysham to say, that had the 300 been inoculated, instead of 90 succumbing to the disease, not above 6 persons would have died ; and 84 persons might have been saved to their parents and the public. Heysham justly complained of the prejudice against the salutary practice of inoculation amongst the vulgar, and that few, very few, could be prevailed upon, either by promises, rewards, or entreaties, to submit to the operation. " No wonder, that in rude, ignorant, and barbarous times, superstition hurried men into the grossest absurdities ; when in a polished and enlightened age, in an age too, when the experience of full twenty years* had clearly demonstrated the utility of inoculation, we see the bulk of mankind ready to sacrifice their children, and all that is dear to them, to a foolish prejudice."

The following Table V. shows the total of deaths in each season :—

TABLE V.

Deaths in	Males.	Females.	Total.	Total of Deaths in each Season.
January	4	7	11	
February	6	4	10	33 Winter.
March	6	6	12	
April	6	3	9	
May	7	10	17	34 Spring.
June	5	3	8	
July	7	7	14	
August	14	5	19	75 Summer.
September	20	22	42	
October	30	23	53	
November	18	20	38	116 Autumn.
December	10	15	25	
Total	133	125	258	

	Males.	Females.	Total.	N.B.—The christenings are by no means accurate, many of the Dissenters not being registered.
Christenings.	102	109	211	

* Lady Mary Wortley Montagu introduced "the engrafting of the small-pox" into England in 1722. It met with virulent opposition at the hands of both doctors and clergy. The Rev. Edward Messey preached a sermon against it, and asserted that "Job's distemper was confluent smallpox, and that he had

These five tables were compiled by Dr. Heysham to illustrate the bills of mortality for 1779. He adopted the same forms in subsequent years, up to the end of December 1787 ; it is not necessary to repeat each year, as the general results of his nine years' observations are recorded in another page.

Dr. Heysham's placing the months of February and March as winter months is not so inconsistent as it appears. March is the most trying month of the year, with cold, north-east winds, and frost.

FOR THE YEAR 1780.—A feeling had got abroad, especially among the political economists, that the population and resources of Great Britain were depreciating very fast, and that we would become an easy prey to our enemies, particularly the French. The data from which these untoward inferences had been drawn were the returns of the window-surveyors, and the books of the custom and excise.* Heysham had the opportunity of showing

been inoculated by the devil !" The Smallpox Hospital in London was founded in 1746. The College of Physicians gave their unanimous sanction to the practice of inoculation in 1754 ; prior to this date, however, Lady Montagu's noble example had been largely followed among the upper ranks.

* The Government, rightly or wrongly, believed in the depopulation of the country, but, instead of trying to remedy such a state of things by sanitary legislation, continued their odious window-tax to make matters worse. In a future page of this volume it will be seen how dreadfully this tax operated on the citizens of Carlisle in 1781 and subsequently. In the history of legislation

the fallacy of these calculations as far as Carlisle was concerned, and thereby helped to cast a doubt on the general data furnished from the country at large by Government officials.

"In the beginning of the year 1780," writes Heysham, " I made an actual, and, I believe, an accurate survey of the two parishes, St. Mary's and St. Cuthbert's,* and found they contained 1148 houses, 1872 families, and 7677 inhabitants." A few months afterwards another survey was made by surveyors for the window-tax, who only returned 815 houses, the difference therefore between the *real* number of houses and the number *returned* to the window-tax was 333. Heysham supposed that if, in ignorance of the real facts, he had taken the 815 houses of the surveyor's report, and multiplied this number by six and two-thirds,† which he looked upon as nearly the number of people in

no more absurd enactment could be found than imposing a tax on the air and light of heaven.

* In this survey the outlying townships are included with the city and suburbs. *Vide* Table I.

† As a rule, Heysham gave six persons to a family household. The assigning four children to each parentage will appear to many readers a somewhat high proportion. On considering the prolificacy of the district, there is no reason, however, for doubting his opinions on this head. The native Cumbrians did well ; and, with their early connubialities, the Irish and Scotch were not far behind in the race, so that all parties contributed their quota to the Carlisle census. The large number of children, so many of whom die in infancy, or under five years of age, greatly tended to increase the tables of mortality. This fact will be noted in another place.

each house, the product would have been 5433 nearly, or 2244 less than the real number, or two-sevenths of the whole.

Only 1 in 34½ nearly of all the inhabitants of Carlisle died this year (1780) in consequence of diseases.

Last year's Bills were confirmed as to women living longer than men, "for between 100 and 103 years old two persons died who were both females; 26 husbands and only 15 wives died, although there are a greater number of wives than husbands in Carlisle." The greatest number of consumptive cases died between 20 and 30 years of age than during any other period of ten years.

FOR THE YEAR 1781.—" People of all ranks, ages, and conditions of life enjoyed an uncommon degree of health during the first three months of this year, for within that period no more than 23 persons died, and of these 15 were either very young children or old and infirm. But about the beginning of April, a very epidemic fever, evidently the *Typhus carcerum*, began to make its appearance." * The smallpox were constantly in town all this year, but 19 only died. Great numbers were inoculated both in the town and country villages.

The difference of the number of deaths of husbands and wives was not near so great as in 1799 and 1780, yet still the deaths

---

* This jail-fever, as described by Dr. Heysham, will be treated in a separate chapter.

of the former exceed those of the latter by two ; for 33 husbands
and only 31 wives have died.

Between 80 and 90 years of age, 5 males and 4 females;
and between 90 and 100, three females died.

During this year 1 in 38⅔ of the inhabitants died of disease.

FOR THE YEAR 1782.—The *Typhus carcerum*, or jail-fever,
which raged with so much violence last year, gradually declined,
and was scarcely to be met with after May.   Sixteen persons
died of it.   Thirty people died of smallpox.   In June of this
year the *Catarrhus contagiosus*, or *Influenza*, became so general
in Carlisle that very few families escaped its influence ; but only
one death occurred.   Heysham entered into the history of the
epidemic, and of its frequent occurrence in Europe in the
eighteenth century.   It seems to have been a very mild disease
in Carlisle, differing little from the common catarrh or cold, except that the febrile symptoms were more constant and rather
more severe.

The mortality of 1782 was only a fraction less than 1781—
namely 1 in 38.   For the first time, the number of deaths of
wives exceeded those of husbands—22 wives against 20 husbands.
The longevity of the people is again marked.   Between 80 and
90 years of age, 5 males and 9 females, and between 90 and
100, 1 male and 2 females, died.   A widow died in her 102d
year.

FOR THE YEAR 1783.—The weather during summer and autumn was "extremely hot and sultry, and there was more thunder and lightning than ever was remembered, even by the oldest person." The prevalence of smallpox led to a general inoculation. By this salutary measure, Carlisle was, in the space of two months, totally freed from a most fatal disorder, then raging in different parts of the county, and destroying 1 in 3 attacked at Whitehaven. The health of Carlisle was otherwise good, and only 1 in 43 of the inhabitants died.

Twenty-nine husbands and 23 wives died this year. Between 80 and 90 years of age, 4 males and 7 females, 6 of whom were widows; and between 90 and 100, 1 male and 1 female died.

Nineteen only fell victims to the smallpox, and 17 of these were children under five years of age.

Apoplexies were remarkably frequent this year, and no less than 9 persons died from them. The numbers of deaths from all diseases were remarkably equal during all the seasons; 47 died in winter, 42 in spring, 45 in summer, and 47 in autumn.

FOR THE YEAR 1784.—In reporting the extreme salubrity of this year, and that only 154 persons died, he calls attention to the fact that in 1779 the number swept off by two diseases only —namely, the smallpox and scarlet fever—was nearly equal to the whole number of deaths in the year, whether occasioned by diseases or accidents.

The present year commenced and ended with the severest and longest-continued frosts ever remembered since the year 1740. The summer, too, was uncommonly cold and wet, and yet was the healthiest season ; only 1 in 50⅓, nearly, died.　In the midst of this healthiness an obstinate skin-disease, Herpes, prevailed, and taxed the skill of the physician and the patience of the lieges affected.

Twenty-nine husbands, but only 20 wives, died this year ; 4 widowers and 24 widows.

Between 80 and 90 years of age, 4 males and 9 females, 8 of whom were widows ; and between 90 and 100, 1 male and 3 females died.

Hitherto the number of males born has exceeded the number of females ; but this year it is the reverse, for 121 males and 153 females have been christened.

FOR THE YEAR 1785.—This year was ushered in by frost of long continuance, and the drought of the spring, and far on to summer, was beyond anything ever remembered.　There was no rain—a very few slight showers excepted—from the month of October 1784 till the 29th July 1785.　Jail-fever, originating among the felons confined in the jail, spread over the town, and 97 persons were affected by it.　The fever was in a milder form than four years previously, and was occasionally attended with relapses.　Only 4 out of the 97 died, and two of these were not seen till remedies were unavailable. As these people lived in nasty lanes, and were huddled together, the small mortality is astonishing ; and the curiosity of the medical reader is excited to know the " reason why," and this the next paragraph in the report explains—" The Dispensary expended upwards of £30 for wine, all of which was consumed by persons affected with the fever."

The Dispensary Committee, of which Dr. Heysham was the ruling mind, had again to adopt strict measures with reference to the smallpox. About 200 persons were inoculated, every one of whom not only recovered, but had the disease in a very favourable manner. Fifty lives, Heysham conjectured, were saved by this general inoculation. 39 died of smallpox this year, who were all under 5 years of age.

As usual, the husbands fared worse than wives. 29 husbands and only 25 wives, 9 widowers and 21 widows, died during the year. The mortality of all the inhabitants was 1 in 37¼ nearly.

Heysham noted an interesting fact as to age affecting mortality—that in 1450 persons from 10 to 20 years old only 2 died. This comparative immunity from death in young folk (that is, after the infantile period) has been frequently witnessed since Heysham's day. The longevity of the Carlisle folk is strikingly seen this year, 14 persons dying between 80 and 90 years of age, and 6 between 90 and 100 years of age. The births were 148 males and 119 females.

FOR THE YEAR 1786.—This year showed the same mortality as 1785 ; and the hottest months were the healthiest.   At two o'clock on the morning of August 11, the shock of an earthquake was felt by many persons in Carlisle and the neighbourhood. The concussion seemed to have extended across the island from Newcastle to Whitehaven, and from the south to the north, including Glasgow and the northern parts of Lancashire.

Measles, in a mild form, was very common, but of the 600 or 700 attacked, only 28 died, the greater part of whom were the children of the poorest class ; 26 were under 5 years of age ; 2 were between 5 and 10 years old.   An old soldier, who had been subject to many vicissitudes of life, died at the advanced age of 105 years.   24 husbands and only 21 wives died this year. The widows again figure largely in the deaths between 80 and 100 years.

FOR THE YEAR 1787.—An order was issued from the Court of Quarter Sessions this year to the different constables in the county of Cumberland to make an actual survey of all the inhabitants of the county.   Dr. Heysham showed the lists delivered to the Quarter Sessions to be erroneous as far as Carlisle was concerned.   The survey of the city was made in the latter end of December 1787, so that it may be presumed that his corrections were made early in 1788.   He found the population of the city, suburbs, and outlying townships of St. Mary's and

St. Cuthbert's to be 3864 males, 4813 females ; or 8677 inhabitants—showing an increase in the population in the space of
eight years of exactly 1000 persons.—*Vide* Table VI.

TABLE VI.

Survey of the two Parishes of Carlisle made by the Constables in December 1787.				The Survey corrected by Dr. Heysham.		
	Males.	Females.	Total.	Males.	Females.	Total.
English Street Quarter	730	1020	1750	801	1050	1851
Scotch Street ,,	423	512	935	423	530	953
Fisher Street ,,	143	222	365	.143	222	365
Castle Street ,,	289	368	657	320	411	731
Abbey Street ,,	319	474	793	340	521	861
The Abbey ,,	...	...	...	20	24	44
Botchergate ,,	259	329	588	259	329	588
Rickergate ,,	319	367	686	319	367	686
Caldewgate ,,	576	705	1281	576	705	1281
Harraby ,,	26	26	52	26	26	52
Carleton ,,	91	81	172	91	81	172
Wreay ,,	...	...	...	60	54	114
Brisco ,,	88	82	170	95	89	184
Botcherby ,,	43	46	89	43	46	89
Upperby ,,	44	48	92	44	48	92
Blackhall ,,	169	151	320	169	151	320
Cummersdale ,,	105	123	228	105	123	228
Persons omitted in various parts of the Town . .	...	...	...	30	36	66
Total . .	3624	4554	8178	3864	4813	8677

E

TABLE VII.

Of the NUMBER of INHABITANTS of Different Ages.

	Under 5 years.	Between 5 and 10 years.	Between 10 and 15 years.	Between 15 and 20 years.	Between 20 and 30 years.	Between 30 and 40 years.	Between 40 and 50 years.	Between 50 and 60 years.	Between 60 and 70 years.	Between 70 and 80 years.	Between 80 and 90 years.	Between 90 and 100 years.	Between 100 and 105 years.	TOTAL.
Within the City and Suburbs	859	731	587	543	1030	733	729	498	375	164	44	5	1	6299
In the Villages .	170	177	128	132	298	144	129	90	63	27	14	5	1	1378
Total in 1780 .	1029	908	715	675	1328	877	858	588	438	191	58	10	2	7677
Total in 1788* .	1164	1026	808	763	1501	991	970	665	494	216	66	11	2	8677
Increase . .	135	118	93	88	173	114	112	77	56	25	8	1	...	1000

He attributed this rapid increase to two general causes : *the salubrity of the place*, and *the increase of trade and manufactures*. The former statement he proved by the births exceeding the deaths to the extent of 489 ; and the latter by an ingress of inhabitants into Carlisle exceeding the emigration out of it during the same period, 511 ; which numbers together make up the increase of 1000.

Inoculation, Heysham was persuaded, had greatly contributed

---

* The Census of 1780 was taken in January ; the Census marked above as 1788 was taken in December 1787 by the Constables, and corrected by Heysham early in 1788. It simplifies matters to look upon the respective enumerations of the inhabitants of Carlisle as being made in January 1780 and January 1788, and corresponds with Dr. Heysham's own declaration in the text of "the space of eight years" marked by an increase of exactly 1000 persons in the population of Carlisle.

to the increase of population, not only in Carlisle, but in the whole county of Cumberland. In the year 1779, when the lower class of inhabitants were extremely averse to the salutary discovery, no fewer than 90 persons died of the natural smallpox ; whereas, when the prejudices of the vulgar greatly diminished, and inoculation got a better chance, only 151 died during the eight succeeding years—an average of not quite 19 in each year. After the institution of the Dispensary, the poor enjoyed the privilege of having their children inoculated gratis—an advantage which they readily embraced.

The mildness of the winter and early spring was remarkable. The *common daisy* was in flower on New Year's Day, and continued in blossom almost the whole year. The *primrose* began to blow on the first of February, and the *colt's-foot* and *barren strawberry* very early in the same month. As the season advanced, the weather was cold, gloomy, and wet, and the rainfall was something extraordinary, yet the year was a healthy one, and the last six months remarkably so. *Seventy-three persons only* died during that period.

With the appearance of smallpox, inoculation became general, and with good effect. Of eighty-four persons inoculated at the Dispensary, all not only survived, but had the disease very favourably.

The jail-fever prevailed this year, and 14 persons fell victims to it. 34 husbands and only 22 wives died. The mortality for the year was 1 in 44 nearly.

TABLE VIII.—DR. HEYSHAM'S TABLE of the DISEASES which caused all the DEATHS in CARLISLE during the Eight Years, 1779, 1781, 1782, 1783, 1784, 1785, 1786, and 1787.*

Disease	Under 5 years	Between 5 and 10 years	Between 10 and 15 years	Between 15 and 20 years	Between 20 and 30 years	Between 30 and 40 years	Between 40 and 50 years	Between 50 and 60 years	Between 60 and 70 years	Between 70 and 80 years	Between 80 and 90 years	Aged 90 and upwards	Of all Ages	Proportion of 10,000 deaths
1. FEBRILE DISEASES—														
Inflammatory Fever	3					1		1					5	31
Nervous "	2	4			4	3	9	15	13	7	2		59	365
Putrid "	5	2	2	1	2	8	5	8	4	5	1		43	266
Jail "	4		2	1	2		2	3					14	87
Mortification		2							1				3	19
Sore Throat							1	2					3	19
Pleurisy					2	4	4	3	3	3			19	118
Stone and Gravel								2	3	3	1		9	56
Rheumatism				2		3		2	2				9	37
Gout								1	2	3			6	25
Smallpox	225	8	5										238	1,474
Measles	28	2	1										31	192
Scarlet Fever	31	4	4										39	241
Thrush	63	2											65	402
Consumption	34	15		10	15	45	34	31	15	15			214	1,325
Worm Fever	19	8											27	167
Flooding					1	2							3	19
Teething	3												3	19
5 other Diseases (A)						1	1	1	1	1			5	31
2. NERVOUS DISEASES—														
Apoplexy					1		2	5	9	11	4		32	198
Palsy							1	1	5	4	3	1	14	87
Fainting						1	1	2	1		1		6	37
Indigestion							1	6	5	8	1		21	130
Convulsions	10												10	62
Epilepsy	1				1		1	1					4	25
Asthma					1			2	9	11	4		27	167
Chincough	18	1											19	118
Looseness	7			1	1	1	1	2	2	1	2		18	111
4 other Diseases (B)							2						5	31

													Total	In 10,000
3. DISEASES OF THE HEART—														
Weakness of Infancy	204												204	1,263
Decay of Age									26	90	84	26	226	1,399
Dropsy		2	2	3	3	5	5	7	12	7	2	1	49	303
Dropsy of the Brain				1	1	1	1	1					5	31
King's Evil					1		1	1					3	19
Venereal Disease							1	1					2	12
Jaundice	3				2		2	2	2	2			13	80
4. LOCAL DISEASES—														
Cancer								1	2	2			5	31
Difficult Delivery													9	56
Unknown Diseases	32	11	5										115	712
8 other Diseases (C)													9	56
Accidents	7	5	2	4	3	4	2	1	1				29	180
GRAND TOTAL	709	74	30	38	79	81	108	94	152	134	89	27	1615	10,000

PROPORTION of DEATHS to POPULATION in CARLISLE.

1779	. .	1 in 30 $\frac{3}{9}$
1780	. .	1 in 34 $\frac{1}{2}$
1781	. .	1 in 38 $\frac{3}{4}$
1782	. .	1 in 38
1783	. .	1 in 43 $\frac{1}{2}$
1784	. .	1 in 50 $\frac{1}{6}$
1785	. .	1 in 37 $\frac{1}{2}$
1786	. .	1 in 37 $\frac{5}{6}$
1787	. .	1 in 44

$$9 \overline{)\ 354}$$
$$39\tfrac{1}{3}$$

With the view of comparison, Dr. Heysham instanced the year 1812.

1812   1 in 40 $\frac{5}{8}$

Population . . . 13,495

Soldiers—55th and 2d Dragoon Guards, exclusive of Wives and Children— } 300

Deaths . . 338) 13,795 (40
            1,352
            ———
             275

SUPPLEMENT to DR. HEYSHAM'S TABLE, containing the DISEASES whereof only One or Two died.

	Under 5 years.	Between 5 and 10 years.	Between 10 and 15 years.	Between 15 and 20 years.	Between 20 and 30 years.	Between 30 and 40 years.	Between 40 and 50 years.	Between 50 and 60 years.	Between 60 and 70 years.	Between 70 and 80 years.	Between 80 and 90 years.	Aged 90 and upwards.	Of all Ages.	Proportion of 10,000 deaths.
1. FEBRILE DISEASES—														
Ague	...	...	...	...	...	...	...	1	...	...	...	...	1	6.2
Inflammation of Stomach	...	...	...	1	...	...	...	...	...	...	...	...	1	6.2
Abscess of the Liver	...	...	...	...	...	...	1	...	...	...	...	...	1	6.2
Miliary Fever	...	...	...	...	1	...	...	...	...	...	...	...	1	6.2
Influenza	...	...	...	...	...	...	...	...	1	...	...	...	1	6.2
(A) of these 5 Diseases	...	...	...	1	1	...	1	1	1	...	...	...	5	31.
2. NERVOUS DISEASES—														
Green Sickness	...	...	...	1	...	...	...	...	...	...	...	...	1	6.2
Colic	...	...	...	...	1	...	...	...	...	...	...	...	1	6.2
Diabetes	...	...	...	...	...	1	...	...	...	...	...	...	1	6.2
Insanity	...	...	...	...	...	1	...	...	...	1	...	...	2	12.4
(B) of these 4 Diseases	...	...	...	1	1	2	...	...	...	1	...	...	5	31.
3. DISEASES OF THE HABIT—														
A discharge of Blood	...	...	...	...	...	...	1	...	...	...	...	...	1	6.2
Costiveness	1	...	...	...	...	...	...	...	...	...	...	...	1	6.2
Suppression of Urine	...	...	...	...	...	...	...	...	1	...	...	...	1	6.2
Obstruction of the Menses	...	...	...	...	...	1	...	...	...	...	...	...	1	6.2
Tumour of the Stomach	Doubtful			...	...	...	...	1	...	...	...	...	1	6.2
Rupture	...	...	...	1	...	...	...	...	...	...	...	...	1	6.2
Ulcer	...	...	...	...	...	...	1	...	1	...	...	...	2	12.4
Ulcer of the Bladder	...	...	...	...	...	...	...	...	1	...	...	...	1	6.2
(C) of these 8 Diseases	1	...	...	1	...	1	2	1	3	...	...	...	9	56.

TYPHUS.

1779	5	1785		9
1780	3	1786		10
1781	48	1787		14
1782	16			
1783	6			9) 119
1784	8		Per Annum	13

TABLE OF DEATHS from SMALLPOX in Carlisle, from a paper enclosed in a letter to Mr. Joshua Milne, Nov. 1, 1812.

1779	90	1785	39
1780	3	1786	1
1781	19	1787	30
1782	30		
1783	19		9) 241
1784	10		26.7

Dr. Heysham summed up the average of the nine years from 1779 to 1787 inclusive, and found that 1 in 39¼ of the inhabitants of Carlisle died annually. " It must be remarked, in the first place, that every infectious and epidemic disease, to which the human body is subject (the plague excepted), prevailed during this period at Carlisle ; and in the second place, that the calculations were made for the first eight years from the number of inhabitants which existed in the beginning of the year 1780 ; the great increase of 1000 not being ascertained till December 1787. Therefore, although the deaths from accidents were not taken into the account for several of the first years, yet, upon the whole, the mortality is stated to be greater than it actually is."—See Table IX.

TABLE IX.

Of the PROPORTION of the DEATHS to the LIVING under Different Ages. From January 1779 to the end of the Year 1787.

			Average of Nine Years.
Under	5 years	...	1 in 12 and 9-11ths nearly.
5 ... 10	„	...	1 in 115 and 2-9ths „
10 ... 15	„	...	1 in 284 and 1-7th „
15 ... 20	„	...	1 in 119 and 3-10ths „
20 ... 30	„	...	1 in 145 and 9-10ths „
30 ... 40	„	...	1 in 100 and 3-5ths „
40 ... 50	„	...	1 in 73 and 5-6ths „
50 ... 60	„	...	1 in 57 nearly.
60 ... 70	„	...	1 in 23 and 9-10ths
70 ... 80	„	...	1 in 10 and 7-8ths
80 ... 90	„	...	1 in 5 and 11-14ths
90 ... 100	„	...	1 in 3 and 13-18ths „

Of all the inhabitants in 1779, 1 in $30\frac{3}{8}$ died annually; in 1780, 1 in $34\frac{1}{2}$; in 1781, 1 in $38\frac{3}{8}$; in 1782, 1 in 38; in 1783, 1 in $43\frac{1}{7}$; in 1784, 1 in $50\frac{1}{6}$; in 1785, 1 in $37\frac{1}{7}$; in 1786, 1 in $37\frac{5}{6}$; in 1787, 1 in 44. The average of the nine years being 1 in $39\frac{1}{4}$ nearly.

N.B.—This Table makes the mortality greater than it actually is, as the calculations from 1779 to 1787 inclusive were made from the number of inhabitants which existed in January 1780; whereas there was an increase of 1000 in that period.

"The deaths which occurred from accidents were, in 1779, 4; in 1780, 3; in 1781, 5; in 1782, 4; in 1783, 3; in 1784, 5; in 1785, 4; in 1786, 2; and in 1787, 2."

From Table IX. it appears that the most healthy period of human life is from 10 to 15 years of age; and that health declines in the following order—namely, between 20 and 30, 15 and 20, 5 and 10, 30 and 40, 40 and 50, 50 and 60, 60 and 70, under 5, 70 and 80, 80 and 90, 90 and 100.

In the month of April 1796 a survey was made of Carlisle by Mr. Johnston, under the direction of the editors of Hutchinson's *History of Cumberland;* and the two parishes of St. Mary and St. Cuthbert were found to contain 1587 houses, 2616 families, and 10,289 inhabitants. It therefore appears that the increase in the population of Carlisle from 1780 to 1796 was 2612, and from 1788 to 1796 of 1612 persons.

CHAPTER IV.

HISTORY OF THE JAIL-FEVER IN CARLISLE—THE FOUNDATION OF THE
CARLISLE DISPENSARY—MEDICAL CASES—HUMAN MONSTROSITY.

IN the beginning of April 1781, there was an outbreak of typhus fever in Carlisle, resembling in character the jail-fever or *Typhus carcerum* of authors. This fever made its appearance in Ricker-gate, a suburban district on the north side, in a house which contained about half-a-dozen very poor families ; the rooms were exceedingly small, and in order to diminish the window-tax, every window that even poverty could dispense with, was shut up : hence stagnation of air, which was rendered still more noxious by the filth and uncleanliness of the people. "One of the persons affected with fever in this house was a weaver, who, on his recovery, went to his usual employment at a large workshop, where he communicated the disease to his fellow-weavers, and from thence the fever spread all over the town." The disease prevailed "amongst the common and lower ranks of people, and more especially those who lived in narrow, close, confined lanes, and in small crowded apartments. It continued for twelve months, and affected adults more frequently than children ; the infirm than the robust; women than men; and the married were more subject to it than the single. It often seized a whole family, and was worse in the suburbs than within the walls of the city."

About 600 persons took the disease—that is, about 1 in 11 or 12 of all the inhabitants of Carlisle,* and 1 in 10 nearly of all who were attacked, died. Of the 52 deaths there were 3 boys, 3 bachelors, 15 husbands, 3 girls, 2 maids, 21 wives, and 5 widows; so that two-thirds of those who succumbed to the fever were married people.

As there was no evidence to show that the fever was imported into the house in Rickergate, the fever was believed to have its origin in this nest of filth and contamination. The same view had been entertained of the disease as observed in jails, or very crowded hospitals, in the two preceding centuries ; hence Dr. Heysham's definition of the epidemic in Carlisle—*Typhus carcerum.*

Dr. Heysham, in 1782, published an essay on the subject— " An account of Jail-Fever or *Typhus carcerum*, as it appeared at Carlisle in the year 1781," in which he states that, as this form of fever was already well known, he would not have obtruded his opinions upon public attention, had not the treatment of the disease which he adopted and successfully pursued appeared to

* Dr. Heysham had ascertained that " in January 1780, there were 6299 inhabitants in Carlisle ; of these 1019 were husbands, 1091 were wives ; 91 were widowers ; 408 were widows ; and the remainder were either children, bachelors, or maids."

differ from what had hitherto obtained in general practice. This difference consisted in the more early application, and in the much freer use, of bark and port wine.

He described the symptoms*—headache, nausea, lassitude, weakness and weariness, dejection of spirits, thirst, disturbed sleep, followed by incoherent talk ; pulse frequent and feeble, tongue dry and brown, and, when thrust out of the mouth for examination, unsteady and tremulous. In the worst cases, those which proved fatal, the pain of the head increased, a putrid colliquative looseness, etc., comes on. "Sometimes *petechiæ* appear in different parts of the body, and in some cases the whole surface of the body is covered with a scarlet efflorescence, which, however, soon disappears. The pulse becomes weaker and quicker, from 130 to 150 strokes in a minute ; the patient is now altogether insensible ; the excretions are voided without consciousness ; he knows not the bystanders ; the delirium is, however, of the low, not of the furious or outrageous kind ; his muscles become flaccid, he gathers his bedclothes, and is affected with *subsultus tendinum*, convulsive startings and twitchings of the whole body, cold extremities; then the livid and cadaverous appearance, ending in death."

---

* Heysham gave Cullen's nosological character of typhus—"*Morbus contagiosus; calor parum auctus; pulsus parvus, debilis, plerumque frequens; urina parum mutata; sensorii functiones plurimum turbatæ, vires multum imminutæ.*"

There was a diarrhœa or cough occasionally in the course of the fever, but no relapse. " Patients died from the 5th or 6th day to the 16th or 17th days. The salutary terminations occurred as frequently on the *non-critical* as on the *critical* days. In one case no visible change for the better took place till the 18th day." Thus the doctrine of critical days could not be applied to this form of fever.

The salutary termination of the disease depended on the constitution of the patient, and the early administration of wine.

The *petechiæ* did not portend imminent danger, nor did a bleeding of the nose ; moreover, Heysham never observed either *petechiæ* or *scarlet efflorescence*, or a *bleeding of the nose*, in patients who began to take the *bark* and *wine* early in the disease.

He believed in the extreme contagiousness of the fever, and " that it was the offspring of filth, nastiness, and confined air in rooms crowded with many inhabitants." He maintained that the *Human Effluvia*, subtle, active, and virulently poisonous, often originated in ships, hospitals, and jails ; in proof of which he instanced the Assizes held at Oxford in the year 1577, when *putrid effluvia* arising from the prisoners at the bar infected a great part of the Court with a pestilential fever, of which upwards of 300 persons died. Also the more melancholy instance at the Sessions of the Old Bailey in 1750, where 100 prisoners were tried, " who were all, during the sitting of the Court, either placed at the bar or confined in two small rooms which opened into the Court. Great numbers present in the Court were almost instantly seized with the jail-fever, and above 40 died of it; but the most remarkable circumstance was, that those only were affected who were on the left-hand side of the Lord Mayor,* a stream of air being directed to that side of the room, in consequence of a window being opened on the other. All on the right-hand side escaped, the *putrid effluvia* being wafted from them to the opposite side."

"In both these instances, it does not appear that the prisoners, either before or after their trial, were particularly affected with any distemper, resembling that which seized so many, and of which they were supposed to have communicated the contagion." To account for the curious fact of the prisoners escaping from the dangers of their own *effluvia*, whilst the fact of their coming into court endangered so many healthy lives, Heysham observed that many of the prisoners had been long confined, and were accustomed to filth and uncleanliness, in conse-

---

* "The persons of chief note who were in Court and died of the fever were Sir Samuel Pennant, Lord Mayor for that year; Sir Thomas Abney, one of the Justices of the Common Pleas; Charles Clarke, Esq., one of the Barons of the Exchequer; and Sir Daniel Lambert, a London Alderman. Of less note, a gentleman at the bar, two students, one of the under-sheriffs, an officer of Lord Chief-Justice Lee, several of the jury, and about forty other persons whom business or curiosity had brought thither."

quence of which the *putrid effluvia* would be generated gradually,
and for a long time be constantly applied to their bodies in small
quantities, till it at length became, as it were, their natural
atmosphere, when they would no more feel its influence than the
tanner perceives the smell of his tanyard, or the *chandler* the
smell of his putrid tallow." He then went on to show that the
human body is possessed of the power of accommodating itself,
or resisting the effects of many active and noxious agencies,
when they are constantly and gradually applied in small quantities, which would injure many of the functions of life, nay, even
in some cases, bring on death, were they given in large doses at
first.   He illustrated this hypothesis by the effects of opium,
hemlock, and tobacco, on the human body, and showed that a
person will in time acquire the habit of taking without danger a
quantity at one dose which would either injure the health, or even
destroy the life, of another person.

The TREATMENT of the fever.—Dr. Heysham relied on
port-wine and *cinchona or bark* given in large quantities.   If
not the first * to advocate stimulants, Heysham prescribed much

* Dr. Heysham, though not original in his views of treating typhus by
stimuli, deserved much credit for setting this example in these northern parts
of the island.   At the beginning of the century (1700), F. Hoffman, the famous
professor at Halle, had recommended nourishing food and good wines for
typhus.   Among British practitioners, Strother of London (1729), Rogers of
Cork (1734), and the better known Huxham of London (1739 and 1757), had all

larger doses than any physician who preceded him in the century. Sir John Pringle, the boldest advocate for wine, seldom gave a bottle in the day, but Heysham ordered from one to two bottles and a half of port in the same period of time, and always with advantage. The doses of bark prescribed by Heysham were also nearly double those which Pringle usually exhibited. In no case did Heysham see any bad effects from the administration of the fullest dose of wine and cinchona. He gave the wine pure, or mixed with cold water for thirst.

" By a copious and liberal use of tonics, cordials, stimulants, or say the wine and bark, the pulse became slower and stronger, the thirst and pain of head abated, the delirium was removed, and the patient got refreshing sleep."

He gave fruit throughout the whole course of the disease, except when contra-indicated by diarrhœa; and this symptom was checked by opiates and astringents.

Ranking or predisposing causes were poor diet, uncleanliness,

advocated the use, more or less, of stimulants ; Sir John Pringle, a high authority, gave bark and serpentaria, and half-a-pint of wine daily ; and Dr. James Lind of Haslar Hospital (1763), and Dr. James Sims of Tyrone (1771-3), shared nearly similar opinions with the President of the Royal Society of London. One year previous to Heysham's detection of the jail-fever at Carlisle, an outbreak of the disease occurred among the Spanish prisoners confined at Winchester, of whom 268 died in three and a half months. Dr. J. Carmichael Smyth, the physician in attendance, condemned bleeding, and gave large quantities of port and Madeira ; in one case two bottles in twelve hours ; and the patient recovered.

intemperance, mental depression ; and these he endeavoured to counteract.

As a preventive of contagion, he recommended a generous diet, and his favourite stimulus, wine, also bark, along with other sanitary measures. He insisted upon clean linen, fresh air directed upon the sick-bed, and through the apartment; in short, thorough cleanliness, as essential to the comfort and cure of the patient.

He dwelt upon the advantage of inspiring his patients with hope, and of avoiding every depressing influence, physical or mental. He condemned the customs prevalent in Carlisle upon the death of any inhabitant :—1st, The tolling of the death-bell, announcing to the world the dissolution ; 2d, The " public cryer," who used to ring his bell and proclaim in every street in a loud, distinct, and melancholy tone of voice, the hour of the deceased's funeral, inviting " all friends and neighbours to attend ;" 3d, Funeral psalms sung by the attendants as they were conducting the corpse through the public streets to the churchyard for inter-ment. " In ages of popish ignorance and superstition," Heysham remarked, " such ceremonies might perhaps be thought conducive to the future happiness and repose of the dead." Knowing the objectionable nature of such lamentations, he sought the aid of Dr. Percy, then Dean of Carlisle, and the Mayor and Corporation, to get them abolished ; and for a time they were, but superstition was too hydra-headed to be crushed *in toto*.

Though the weather was held to be inoperative as a cause of the fever of 1781, it should be stated that the spring of the year was mild and temperate ; the summer " warm, dry, and serene ;" the autumn warm, and the winter tolerably mild, or Heysham could not have gathered the common wild daisy (*Bellis perennis*) on Christmas day.

Nowhere, as a physician, did Dr. Heysham display more character and firmness of purpose than in his advocacy of wine and stimulants in the treatment of typhus. The disease, nay, the very name of fever, was associated with high action, furious pulse, and hot burning skin ; and everybody looked upon such a condition as only to be mastered by bleeding and depletive measures. His acting so contrary to the recognised doctrines of the medical schools of his epoch, as well as the popular beliefs, showed that he had made observation, and not empirical views, his principles of guidance in the treatment of fever. Happily for himself, as well as his patients, the practice he recommended on truly rational grounds was highly successful. So long and persistent had " the starving system " prevailed, along with bleeding, that any other plan was looked upon as highly culpable, if not heinous to a degree. Nearly fifty years had passed over after Heysham's pamphlet was issued—say 1830 or later—before physicians would venture upon the use of wine in fevers ; and then it was no easy matter to indoctrinate the great majority of practitioners with the

F

new views of treatment. Though not the first in Britain, Heysham was assuredly foremost in the North of England to introduce the stimulating mode, and may be said to have been half-a-century in advance of his own times. He deserved more credit than he ever got for making so bold a stand against popular prejudices, and the medical experience that would admit of no exception to bloodletting as a sheet-anchor in the treatment of fevers. It required the philosophical acumen of Alison of Edinburgh, and the practical mind of Graves in Dublin, to shake off the shackles of dogmatic medicine, and to lay down a more rational recognition of the forms of febrile diseases *quoad* treatment. The best proof of the rarity of the stimulating treatment urged by Heysham in 1781, may be found in the words addressed to his Practice of Physic class by Dr. Graves some years ago : " If," said he, " you are at a loss for an epitaph to be placed on my tomb, here is one for you : He fed fevers."

FOUNDATION OF THE CARLISLE DISPENSARY.

The increasing numbers of the sick poor who sought the gratuitous medical services of Dr. Heysham made it imperative upon him to have a larger room than the one attached to his lodgings in St. Cuthbert's Lane, and this led him to think of a public medical institution for the destitute poor of the city. He mentioned his views to Dean Percy of Carlisle, and some of the wealthier classes. The former provided Dr. Heysham with a room attached to one of the prebendal residences, then approached from Castle Street by a narrow lane. Subscriptions were got up, and the Public Dispensary was fairly established on July 1, 1782. To Dr. Heysham is due the entire honour of founding this excellent institution. He was also its first physician. The friends who helped him most in this good work were the Earl of Surrey, then member of Parliament for the city, and afterwards Duke of Norfolk; the bishops of Carlisle, Clonfert, and Dromore; and Messrs. Dacre, Losh, and Liddell. The Dean and Chapter were liberal supporters; and each year, through Heysham's active exertions, the subscriptions of the county families and wealthier manufacturers of the city greatly increased. In the first year 390 patients appeared on the books of the Dispensary, and during the first fourteen years of its operations no less than 11,382 persons shared in the benefits of the charity. Dr. Heysham continued to take deep interest in the welfare of this institution, and is said to have written all the annual reports that were published till the year 1818.

In setting forth the advantages of the Dispensary, he held that £100 a-year might be so managed as to communicate relief to thousands, and that in no other way could money go so far, or charity impart happiness with equal efficacy, or to the like extent. According to his calculation, there were upwards of 4000 inhabit-

ants supported by daily wages, from which little was ever laid
up, so that sickness always found these unprovided for any
extraordinary expense.

In the first report of the Carlisle Dispensary, and written by
Dr. Heysham, embracing the period from July 1, 1782, to July
1, 1783, it is said that 26 cases of jail-fever were admitted to the
benefits of the institution.   All were treated with bark (cinchona)
wine, and considerable doses of opium, and all recovered.   In the
Dispensary, year 1783-84, there were 37 cases of jail-fever, and
in 1784-85, 43 cases of the same fever.   Very early in January
of the year 1785 the jail-fever originated among the felons of the
jail, and then traversed the city, and continued to rage almost
the whole of the year.   In January, February, and March, there
were 4 cases each month.   April had 3 ; May and June each
showed 8 cases ; in July there were 10, in August 15, in September 19, and in October and November there were 11 cases
each month.   The disease was not so virulent as in 1782.
Petechiæ and hemorrhagies were seldom observed.   A greater
portion of children were affected.   Relapses were much more
frequent.   He gave opium early in the disease (1785), and in
large quantities the moment he felt sure of the disease being
" putrid fever."   There were 9 deaths in all in the city out of the
97 cases affected in the 11 months of 1785.   In further Dispensary reports, up to the year 1793, jail-fever occupies a

prominent place ; but the disease had evidently become a much milder disease, and still more amenable to treatment. Thus, in the report 1786-87, there were 59 cases of jail-fever ; in 1787-88 no less than 252 cases, of which 14 died ; in 1788-89, 69 cases ; in 1790-91, 123 cases ; in 1791-92, 158 cases; in 1792-93, there were 123 cases.

Dr. Heysham published, in the *Medical Commentaries* for 1780, vol. vii. p. 349, a " Remarkable Cure of Epilepsy and Dysphagia Spasmodica ;" and in the same volume, p. 359, a case of Epilepsy cured by *Cuprum ammoniacum*, in half-grain doses twice a-day. This preparation of copper seems to have been a favourite remedy in Heysham's hands for all nervous complaints, *ex. gr.* St. Vitus' dance. In his Bills of Mortality for 1782 he gave " an account of a peculiar and painful affection of the *Antrum maxillare*, which, upon being opened, contained three insects." This case led to a great war of words between the Doctor and a Carlisle surgeon, but added nothing to what had been observed by Dr. Fothergill (*Medical Observations and Inquiries*, vols. iii. and v.) Other isolated medical or surgical cases recorded by Dr. Heysham hardly deserve to be noticed in this memoir.

History of a Human Monstrosity.

On the 26th May 1788, Mary Clarke, aged 26 years, and the mother of six children, some of whom were healthy and others unhealthy, was delivered of a living female child,* the strange appearance of whose head alarmed the midwife, who called in Dr. Heysham within an hour after delivery. The doctor found the bones of the upper part of the skull wanting, and, instead of a brain, a large reddish-brown excrescence projecting a little over the integuments towards the forehead, and extending over the root of the nose. He thought he could perceive the division of the two hemispheres of the brain, and likewise the division of the cerebrum from the cerebellum. On raising this substance, the child began to cry, and started as if influenced by an electric shock. The infant was full-grown, and seemed in perfect health ; her limbs were plump, firm, and well-proportioned, and she moved them with apparent agility. The external organs of sense were also perfect. The eyes were full and lively, and the vision seemed perfect. She swallowed well, and took sufficient food, but sometimes during the act of swallowing started a little. She lived from 8 A.M. on Monday, May 26th, till 5 A.M. on the Sunday (June 1st) following, five days and twenty-one hours, and then expired. After the second day she had convulsions occasionally. During the greater part of her brief existence a thin

* The case is narrated in Hutchinson's *History of Cumberland*, vol. ii. p. 676. The medical reader will find it described in the *Memoirs of the Manchester Literary and Philosophical Society*, vol. v. Part ii. p. 496. Dr. John Hull, in a paper read to the said society (Nov. 28, 1800), " On the Nervous System of Different Animals," discussed the physiological bearings of Dr. Heysham's case.

watery fluid, slightly tinged with blood, escaped from the excrescence, which greatly diminished its bulk, and reduced it one-half before death, whilst the surface of the said excrescence was beginning to put on an appearance of mortification.

Such were the conditions observed during the child's life; but an examination after death revealed more extraordinary facts than the mere external appearances indicated. Dr. Blamire and Mr. Charles Farish aided Dr. Heysham in the *post-mortem* inquiry.

The bones which constitute the upper and lateral regions of the head were wanting, and the substance, or excrescence, was found to consist only of membranes, blood-vessels, and several bags, one of which was as large as a nutmeg, the rest of different sizes, and smaller. These bags, or cysts, were filled with a brownish-coloured fluid, that escaped with force on the cysts being punctured. There was not the least appearance of *cerebrum, cerebellum,* or any *medullary* substance whatever; in less technical language, neither the great nor the small brain, nor any brain-substance. The spinal cord, or marrow, had a natural appearance, but did not seem to have been connected with the parts above described.

Dr. Heysham was led to infer—1st. That the fluid discharged from the excrescence during the life of the infant, and which produced the great diminution of its bulk, was occasioned by the

rupture or erosion of cysts, similar to those which remained sound
and full after death.

2d. That the living principle, the nerves of the trunk and
extremities, sensation, and motion, may exist independent of, and
that the natural, vital, and animal functions may be performed without, the brain. And as the external organs of sense—namely, the
eyes, the nose, the tongue, and the ears—all seemed perfect, may we
not, therefore, suppose that the optic, the olfactory, the gustatory,
and the auditory nerves (belonging to the senses), may exist independent of, and unconnected with, either the brain or spinal marrow ?

The Doctor was content with describing this extraordinary
case, leaving others to deduce from it such conclusions as the
appearances observed might be thought to warrant. A fat,
plump, and vigorous child living very nearly six days, and
correctly performing all the ordinary functions pertaining to
infantile life without a brain, or even particle of brain matter, was
a phenomenon well calculated to excite surprise amongst the
uneducated, and not less to puzzle the best informed in science.
No more uncommon instance of fœtal development passing into
extra-uterine life, and for six days manifesting active organic
functions, is to be found in the records of medical history from
that day to the present time. No wonder it is cited both on
account of its rarity and the many physiological considerations
involved in its study.

The anatomy of the brain, and the spinal cord connected above with the brain, and occupying the channel formed by the bones of the spine as low as the loins, was only broadly indicated, whilst the functions of these nervous centres were but little understood in 1788 ; so far, however, as was known, Dr. Heysham reasoned correctly as to the facts observed by him in the case of Mary Clarke's child. It is to be regretted that he did no more than note the conditions of the child, when the case itself afforded a great opportunity for physiological inquiry.

The nervous system was a great puzzle till Sir C. Bell discovered the functions of the roots of the nerves in 1811. Nearly fifty years after Heysham saw the brainless child, Dr. Marshall Hall opened out a new mine of physiological doctrine by experimenting on animals previously reduced to a condition of life resembling that of the child Clarke—namely, by suspending the action of the brain, whilst the functions of the spinal cord were allowed to continue in force. Had Heysham worked the ground lying at his feet, and been possessed of a microscope, he might have demonstrated the fibrillæ or minutest elements of the nerves, and their mode of termination in the encephalon, and helped to unravel some of the intricate problems in biological science.* To trace the mode in which the will conveys its dicta

* That which Dr. Heysham overlooked in 1788 the writer of these pages had the good fortune to discover in 1841 in a child of monstrous formation. *Vide Edinburgh Medical and Surgical Journal,* vol. lx. p. 330.

to the muscles, and is responded to with the quickness of thought ; to ascertain how the instinctive or involuntary acts are manifested independently of the will ; and to note those intimate relations between the nervous centres and the nutritive functions of the body, were of deep interest to the professional mind.   A full and eliminative inquiry into the anatomical and physiological history of the brainless infant would also have helped the cause of psychology, and prepared the English mind for the newer doctrines of an age in which philosophical thought has come to supersede the crude speculations of the past, and sound deductions to take the place of theological supposition and dogma.

Heysham's case,[*] of such interest in the history of human genesis, let insight into Nature's operations, and showed what odd formations might arise if the threads of life were not correctly woven together in the web that constitutes the entity—normal and symmetrical man.   It proved that there were starting points or nuclei of development, from which the formation of organic

* It is curious to note that Carlisle in 1788 yielded a monstrosity in the shape of a brainless child, who lived nearly six days ; and that a child was born about ten miles distant in 1841, in possession of a brain, but without a spinal cord, whose respiration could not be sustained for a moment : both cases stand unparalleled in teratology.   As if Cumberland had not done enough in this way, a child was born near Dalston, five miles west of Carlisle, about 1859, with the smallest possible amount of brain ; it lived three months, and died of internal disease.   The brain of this child, and also its facial features, bore the closest resemblance to the simian class of animals.

structures proceed, and that if a hitch or hiatus occurs, as in the child Clarke, the brain and its suitable bony covering may be replaced by a lot of small bags containing fluid—a miserable substitute for nervous matter, or rather no substitute at all.

The unprofessional reader will gather from the case under discussion, that the ordinary nutritive functions and locomotion of the body do not rest with the brain proper, but with the spinal cord or the nervous substance that is attached to the brain above and extends downwards to the loins, giving forth nerves in every direction, that become interlaced with another portion of the nervous system called the *Sympathetic*, distributed among the viscera of the body. The functions of the brain are of a higher order, marking the sentient and intellectual being, guiding the actions of life, and affording what claims man can be said to possess to immortality.

Considering the progress that philosophic thought had made, and that Locke and Hartley, both of whom were physicians, had brought their professional knowledge to bear upon metaphysics, it is remarkable that Heysham had so little to say on the relations of the brainless infant to psychology. Hartley's theory of vibrations in the white substance of the brain being the immediate cause of sensation, was an attempt to explain, on strictly anatomico-physiological grounds, the *modus operandi* of thought—the sphinx or riddle of philosophers in all ages. This opinion of Hartley's was well calculated to claim the attention of his medical brethren, and seemed particularly relevant to the case *sub judice ;* but Heysham had either been unacquainted with the writings of Hartley, and the doctrines of Bonnet, the Genevese naturalist, or he had deemed it prudent to abstain from any expression that would link his medical reasonings with the materialistic views of Hobbes and Hume, then held to be so dangerous and heterodox.   Though Hartley was classified with the materialists, as all innovators on established forms of thought are apt to be, he was a believer, and a highly religious person, whom Coleridge describes as—

> " He of mortal kind
> Wisest ; the first who marked the ideal tribes
> Up the fine fibres to the sentient brain."

CHAPTER V.

IN the first ten years of his residence in Carlisle (1778 to 1788), Dr. Heysham had done more perhaps than any one of his medical predecessors in the place, to advance its strictly medical interests, and to promote its sanitary welfare. He had made two surveys of the city and its suburbs and village-parochial districts, and numbered the houses, the families, and the population therein. Along with the census he had collected the numbers of births and deaths, the ages and conditions of the people ; and by classifying the causes of and circumstances attendant on the death-rate, had framed bills of mortality for each year.

He had founded a public Dispensary, and laid down good rules for its guidance and future success, and hesitated not for many years to take upon himself a large share of its medical responsibility.

In his wish to extend the area of medical knowledge, and to make his study and observation of disease of historical utility, he had published a valuable essay on jail-fever, and described a deeply-interesting case of human monstrosity.

Professional work, though daily urgent, was not the sole occupation of his mind ; in the midst of numerous private and public engagements he found leisure to study the natural history of Cumberland.

Dr. Heysham ceased to tabulate his observations on the bills of mortality after 1788. No reason has ever been assigned for this ; it may have been owing to his increasing practice, or greater partiality for natural history ; probably he was influenced by a more potent charm than scientific inquiries in the person of Miss Coulthard, only daughter and heiress of Alderman Thomas Coulthard, a rich tanner, who had twice occupied the mayoralty of Carlisle. He was married to Elizabeth Mary Coulthard in London on 4th May 1789. He was in his thirty-sixth year, his wife was in her twenty-fourth year. Mrs. Heysham bore a family of four sons and three daughters to her husband. She died on 30th May 1803. Of her sons, John Coulthard Heysham died in infancy ; William, lieutenant and adjutant of the 53d Bengal Native Infantry, died 13th October 1825, aged twenty-nine years ; Thomas Coulthard Heysham, a distinguished naturalist, died in Carlisle, 6th April 1857, aged sixty-six years ; James Heysham, lieutenant of the navy, died at Borren's Hill, Carlisle, 10th May 1870. Of his daughters, Mary Heysham died 28th May 1808, aged fourteen years ; Isabella, who became the wife of Mr. G. G. Mounsey, of Castletown, Carlisle, died 14th May 1848, leaving numerous issue.   The only survivors are the Rev. John Heysham, M.A., Vicar of Lazonby, Cumberland, and Miss Anna Heysham of Carlisle.

Dr. Heysham, on his marriage, took a three-storey house immediately opposite his old lodgings in St. Cuthbert's Lane : there he and his wife lived happily, and brought up their family in a manner commensurate with their good position in society.   He was affectionately attached to his children.

Dr. Heysham was a naturalist in the true acceptation of the term, and did more than any other person to make the natural history of Cumberland generally known.   His penchant for the study of animated nature arose in early life amidst the woods and dales of Westmoreland, and along the pleasant shores of Morecambe Bay, where he loved to wander and enjoy the picturesque scenery around.   Being skilled in the use of the bow and arrow, his rural walks were made subservient to his ornithological pursuits, and these of all others were the most favoured in his natural-history career.   If his first steps were juvenile and amateur-like, the knowledge gained of anatomical forms, by his medical studies, gave a fresh colouring and precision to his observations.   He soon made himself known as a naturalist, and far beyond the Carlisle district.   He was elected an Associate of the Linnæan Society,

London, at the second meeting of the said society held at the Marlborough Coffee-House in March 1788. The writer is not aware if Heysham contributed any papers to the "Linnæan;" there is no record of such in the Society's "Transactions;" and as he died before the publication of the monthly "Proceedings," there is no obituary notice of him by the Society.

Persons residing in Cumberland and Westmoreland, who met with birds of doubtful plumage, or rare specimens, or who had marked any deviation from the usual habits and manifestations of animals, used to consult Heysham. In this way he enjoyed the double advantage of his own observations and the experience of others. He compared notes with fellow-workers over a wide area of country, so that every division of the northern district came to be explored—the high peaks of the fells, the green dale-land, the marshes, rivers, seabord, and, in fact, the sea itself, from Burgh-on-Sands and the Scottish shore to Barrow-in-Furness, Lancashire. As books were scarce and dear, a local and scientifically educated authority of Heysham's stamp was sought for and highly prized by less favoured promoters of natural history. Distance of locality counted nothing with enthusiastic minds; and if Heysham would walk twenty miles to see a nest, others would travel twice the distance to take counsel of a proved leader in the science they loved so well.

Though ready to investigate both land and marine animals by

the more or less imperfect lights of Linnæus and Buffon, the authorities of one hundred years ago, his special study was ornithology
and some divisions of entomology. He collected great numbers
of birds, also their eggs and nests, and preserved the best *generic*
specimens, with which to compare any additional examples that
might come in his way. He adopted the same practice in other
departments of the animal kingdom ; and being favoured with
the friendship of such gentlemen as Sir James Graham, the first
Baronet of Netherby, and Mr. John Losh of Woodside, who took
interest in his pursuits, he was enabled to gather a rich harvest
of facts in natural history. These facts became of import at an
earlier date than was expected, owing to an application being
made to Heysham by Mr. William Hutchinson, about to undertake a History of Cumberland,* to furnish "a Catalogue of Cumberland Animals" for the proposed work. Heysham was the only
man in the county acquainted with the animal tribes, so that his
co-operation in the work was not only of import, but essential and
imperative, seeing that a history of Cumberland devoid of infor-

---

* Heysham, though he possessed the records of fifteen years' observation,
would hardly have gone to press on his own account, knowing, as he would do,
that Cumberland folk were not much given to any form of reading, and that they
would rather borrow than buy a volume. As very few people cared a straw for
natural history, it would have been unwise to incur so great an expense as
that of publishing an essay on the Fauna of Cumberland. His observations
filled 53 pages of double-lined quarto in Hutchinson's *History.*

mation on the natural products and fauna of the county would
have been manifestly imperfect.

Heysham entered with spirit upon the work assigned him by
the editor, and the result of his labours up to 1793 or 1794 is to
be found recorded in the first pages of Hutchinson's *History of
Cumberland.* In glancing at Heysham's public contributions, the
writer must content himself with a few general notes, exemplifying
the originality of his observations, or the more instructive generic
data of his work.

In his classification of the Cumbrian fauna, Heysham relied
mainly upon the *Systema Naturæ* of Carl Linnæus ; Thomas
Pennant's *British Zoology* (1761-77) ; and John Latham's
General Synopsis of Birds (1781). Along with the technical
description he gave the local nomenclature for each species, so
that, whilst his catalogue was scientific in character, it was no less
accessible to the meanest capacity. It is worthy of special note
that Heysham only recorded what he had himself seen and
investigated : his observations necessarily bear a high value,
compared with those of the mere compiler and copier of other
men's labours. He went carefully through the whole animal
kingdom ; beginning with the quadrupeds, and passing down the
zoological scale, he catalogued every species known to exist in
Cumberland. His notes appended to each description rendered
the whole compendium readable, instructive, and locally interest-

ing.   His work bespeaks labour, research, and a painstaking accuracy, all the more creditable that it was undertaken on behalf of the interests of science.

The narrative of his natural history experiences, as found in Hutchinson's *History of Cumberland*, comes down to 1794 or thereabouts ; since which time, it is hardly needful to say, changes have taken place in the county greatly affecting the condition of the people, and correlatively the natural habits of the zoological genera—be they the casual bird visitors or indigenous tribes observed within its area eighty years ago.   Significant as is the contrast between the primitive living and bucolic pastimes of Cumbrians at the close of the last century, and the reigning fashion of to-day ;   more widely apart, however, may be said to stand the relations of the winged tribes to their former rendezvous and habitations.   To avoid the haunts of men and the wanton savagery of indiscriminate shooters, abandonment of the old grounds, or dispersion, has become an instinctive necessity with the rarer species, failing which, nothing less than annihilation awaits them in England.   Nowhere, perhaps, in the whole range of English ornithology, could a more striking example of this opinion be found than on Newtown Common, within a mile and a half of Carlisle.   Suburban extension, the inroads of the factory system upon rural life, and the depredations of poachers, have rendered a locality that was unusually rich in ornithology in Heysham's day, a complete waste to all but the sparrow and common hedgerow birds.

CLASS I. QUADRUPEDS.—In treating of the *genus* Deer, Heysham states, "The stag or red deer (*Cervus elaphus*,[*] Linn.) may be said to range, almost in a state of nature, in the forests and hills of Martindale, in the neighbourhood of Ullswater." In the same locality were to be seen a few examples of the wild cat, then rapidly disappearing, and now unheard of.

The black rat was becoming rare, having been expelled from the county by the brown rat. Oddly enough, Heysham had a specimen of the black rat "perfectly white" in colour. However incongruous this statement may appear of a specific black animal showing entirely white, it is quite reconcileable with well-ascertained facts in zoology. Man himself presents as great a variety of colour, and what can be more antipodal in external character than the black negro, and the albino—the latter exemplar of the human race being by no means so rare as the white coloured specimen of the black rat. In connection with colour, it may be noted that Heysham had a mole presented to him by William Dacre of Kirklinton of a fine cream colour.

---

[*] Claphus is likely to be an error of spelling for Elaphus, the designation of the red deer by modern writers being *Cervus elaphus*, in honour, it may be supposed, of Aristotle's Ἔλαφός. Linnæus gets the credit of naming it *Cervus vulgaris*. The animal has a long list of synonyms.

CLASS II. BIRDS.—The *Sea Eagle* used to build in the rocks which surround the lake of Ullswater, and the great trout, upwards of ten pounds in weight, of that lake had been taken out of its nest. " Its food is principally fish ; which it takes as they are swimming near the surface, by darting itself down upon them."

The *White-tailed Eagle* was found among the rocks in the neighbourhood of Keswick. A young one taken in Borrowdale was presented to Dr. Law of Carlisle, afterwards Bishop of Elphin ; it lived nineteen years, but the characteristic white tail did not appear till it was six years old.

The *Peregrine Falcon* " breeds constantly every year in a rock near the cascade at Gilsland, or in another high rock six miles from that place, near a public-house called Twice-brewed Ale, on the road from Carlisle to Newcastle." It was near this rock (fifteen miles from Carlisle) that Heysham watched a female falcon constantly upon the wing for five hours ; then it perched and he shot it. Had he lived in the days of Queen Elizabeth, he would have paid dearly for his shot, as the female peregrine, in the language of " falconrie," was called the falcon *par excellence*, and claimed for the royal preserves. Heysham held it to be the most destructive of game of any bird in Cumberland ; later observers fully confirm his view as to the daring and ferocity of this falcon.—(*Vide* Mr. Thompson's paper in *Magaz. Zool. and Botan.* vol. ii. p. 53 ; and Selby's *Ornithology*.)

Hen-harriers.—Linnæus was of opinion that the birds commonly known as hen-harriers and ringtail were of different species; the former he designated *Falco cyaneus*, the latter *Falco pyargus*. Pennant and Latham adopted his views. On the other hand, Brisson, Ray, and Willoughby, considered the hen-harrier male, and the ringtail female, as the male and female birds of one species, known to modern writers as *Circus cyaneus*. Seeing such great names opposed to each other led Heysham to exercise uncommon vigilance. Having discovered, in the year 1783, three nests of the ringtail and hen-harrier on Newtown Common, about a mile and a half from Carlisle, he watched the habits of the birds very closely during the incubated periods of 1783 and 1784. In June 1785 he had also three nests on the same common ; and having entrapped the birds, satisfied himself and others that the birds were male and female, and not distinct species, thus confirming Ray and Willoughby's opinions. Heysham's narrative of his observations is very interesting, and the nature of the evidence adduced by him proved irresistible to Latham, and fairly settled the point at issue.

Merlin.—" Mr. Pennant says the merlin is a bird of passage, and does not breed in England, which is a mistake; it breeds in Cumberland, and remains with us the whole year." Heysham proved this by three nests on Rockcliff Moss, and by obtaining both the male and female birds. He saw a merlin strike a blackbird ; and one day in February (1793) he got a fine cock partridge, which this bird had killed the moment before.

The *Butcher-bird* or Great Shrike (*Lanius excubitor* of Linnæus) is a "beautiful and scarce bird.* I have only met with three or four specimens. In spring and summer it imitates the notes of other birds, by the way of decoying them within reach, that it may destroy them."

The *Carrion-crow* he held to be more numerous in the north of England than in any country of the world, and as destructive to young ducks and chickens as any species of hawk. He asked for the revival of an ancient statute (8 Eliz. c. 15), by which churchwardens could levy an assessment and pay for the heads of "old crowes, choughs, or rooks," and numerous birds of known destructive propensities. At the time he wrote, some parishes in Westmoreland paid so much a head for house-sparrows, and of other birds of no better repute.

The *Jay* stands alone among British birds in feeding entirely upon vegetables, according to Heysham.

The *Cuckoo*, it was ascertained, was migratory in habit. He had difficulty in distinguishing the sex by external colours. He

---

* The Butcher-bird, a native of Norway and Sweden, is extremely rare in Britain. In October 1865 Mr. Jackson Gillbanks, of Whitefield House, shot one near the base of Skiddaw. In the same month one was captured alive by some boys in the market-place of Wick, Caithness. It constitutes the *Lanius cinereus* of Gesner and Aldrovandus.

had seen the cuckoo's egg, and also two eggs in the nests of several small birds—viz. water-wagtail, hedge-sparrow, and tit-lark, but most frequently in the last named ; moreover, he had seen the young cuckoo fed by the titlark.

The common *Kingfisher*, the nest of which had occupied the fancies of Pliny and other ancient writers, and whose plumage had been specially noted by Englishmen on account of its beauty, was found by Heysham to have no nest at all ; the eggs being placed on the bare mould at the extremity of a narrow channel, eighteen inches long, in the banks of the river Peterill. The eggs of the kingfisher and water-ouzel are alike in colour, and nearly so in size. Heysham walked ten miles from home to the banks of the Roe, to see the nest of the water-ouzel.

The *Bohemian* or *Waxen Chatterer* only visits Cumberland occasionally. Great numbers of this beautiful bird were killed in the north of England in the year 1787. Its horny appendages on the tips of the secondary feathers, being of the colour of the very finest red scaling-wax, and other peculiarities, distinguished this bird from all others. At Keswick, Temple-Sowerby, and near Carlisle, specimens were obtained, and Sir Henry Liddell, Bart., sent one to Heysham from Ravensworth in Northumberland.

The *Martins* (*Hirundo urbica, riparia*, and *apus*) engaged much of his attention—their migration, mode of building, etc.

He cited a series of meteorological observations, both of his own
and of Mr. J. Mackenzie of Brampton, with the view of showing
the exact temperature of the air at the times when these martins
appeared and disappeared, and of testing the then disputed point
of migration on the part of these birds. His observations were
conclusive as to their migratory character. Of the Cumberland
birds which migrate, Heysham remarked, but " thirty-eight appear
in the spring, and depart either in the autumn or beginning of
winter, and forty-three appear during the winter, and depart in
the spring." He used invariably, in the spring months, to watch
night and morning, if not oftener in the day, for the arrival of the
swallows, martins, redbreasts, etc.

In 1790 the *Pheasant* and *Blackcock* were rare in Cumberland. Sir J. Graham of Netherby and others were trying to introduce the pheasant—marvellously abundant in the present day.
The blackcock was at the time most seen on the Netherby estate ;
and, singularly enough, there was an annual brood upon Newtown
Common, about a mile and a half from Carlisle. This Newtown
Common seems to have been a wild aviary to Heysham ; and so
different were the genera of birds found upon its waste land, that
it is difficult to account for their habitats being alike, as well as
their numbers being so great.

WATER-BIRDS.—Of the *Common Heron* (*Ardea cinerea* of
Temminck and Latham) Heysham relates a curious history, based

on observations made at Dallam Tower, in Westmoreland :—
" There were two groves adjoining to the park, one of which for
many years had been resorted to by a number of herons, who
there built and bred.   The other was one of the largest rookeries
in the country.   The two tribes lived together for a long time
without disputes.   At length, the trees occupied by the herons,
consisting of some very fine old oaks, were cut down in the spring
of 1775, and the young brood perished by the fall of the timber !
The parent birds immediately set about preparing new habitations, in order to breed again ; but as the trees in the neighbourhood of their old nests were only of a late growth, and not
sufficiently high to secure them from the depredations of boys,
they determined to effect a settlement in the rookery.   The rooks
made an obstinate resistance ; but, after a very violent contest,
in the course of which many of the rooks, and some of their
antagonists, lost their lives, the herons at last succeeded in their
attempt, built their nests, and brought out their young."

The next season the same contests took place, and victory
was again in favour of the heavy battalions.   After this the rooks
relinquished possession of that part of the grove, and, retiring to
a respectable distance, kept the peace towards their betters.

Heysham observes—" This bird (heron), which is now seldom
or ever seen upon a table, was, in former times, esteemed very
delicate food ;" in proof of which he quotes the following prices

of birds from the twenty-seventh year of the reign of Edward I. :
—A fat cock to be sold at three-halfpence, a goose for fourpence,
a partridge for three-halfpence, a pheasant for fourpence, a heron
for sixpence, a plover for a penny, a swan for three shillings, two
woodcocks for three-halfpence, a fat lamb, from Christmas to
Shrovetide, for sixteenpence, and all the year after for fourpence,
Looking to the list of prices of birds sold at Carlisle in 1796, or
five centuries later, the reader will ascertain the difference of the
two periods by multiplying Edward's prices by ten, to gain the
value of victuals in the middle of George the Third's reign in
northern England.

The writer reluctantly passes over what Heysham records of
the dunlin, dotterel, spotted rail, little auk, northern diver, and the
disputed points in the history of the goosander and dun-diver, and
the instances of peculiar apathy manifested by the corvorant.
Before leaving the ornithological division, note should be made of
the fact laid down by Heysham, that in several species of birds,
where the male plumage differs materially from the female, as in
the blackcock and grey hen, hen-harrier and ringtail, all the young
birds, whether male or female, resemble the female more than
they do the male.

Heysham said but little of the REPTILES : he is much more
discursive on FISHES. He describes the angel-fish taken near St.
Bees in 1793, and gives a drawing of it when dried and preserved

for the purposes of a show.   His history of the marine fishes is
ample enough, and embraced all that was known in his time. He
discusses the Salmonidæ at great length, as all anglers and
naturalists have done from " time immemorial ; " and of course saw
strong reasons to find fault with the provisions of the several acts
passed by the Legislature for the protection of the salmon brood.
The writer has too much regard for his reader to think of tres-
passing on salmon ground, so fertile of disputation and endless
unscientific *palaver*.   Heysham's opinions on every subject he
touched are worth attentive consideration ; and nothing more
need be said to induce those in search of *Salmoniana* to peruse
the record of his experiments in the Eden and other Cumberland
rivers, than which no better salmon rivers can be met with in
England.

As the Linnæan system of classification prevailed beyond the
eighteenth century, it is not to be supposed that Heysham's
generic views are strictly in accordance with the opinions held
to-day; his description of species, however, may be thoroughly
relied upon.   Terrestrial animals found pretty nearly their proper
places in the zoological scale, as their anatomy, functions, and
habits, were more patent in character.   This could hardly be
said of the denizens of the deep, which were looked upon as of
one flesh, and that flesh fishy.   The fish swims, so do the whale
and the minnow ; hence arose the doctrine that all were fish that

swam in the sea ; and the classification of the Mammal Cetacea
with the cold-blooded fishes.

All that Dr. Heysham publicly recorded of his natural history
observations, as far as the writer can ascertain, is to be found in
Hutchinson's *History of Cumberland;* yet there is no doubt of his
having done much more in this broad field of inquiry after 1795,
the date of the county history. It is said that he kept his ther-
mometrical records as late as 1830 ; and it is highly probable
that he left numerous manuscripts on these and kindred subjects,
which came into the possession of his son, Thomas Coulthard
Heysham, whose penchant for natural history was quite equal to
his own. Now, there is reason to believe that when Mr. T. C.
Heysham, in his latter years, threw into the fire bundles of his
own papers, containing valuable researches in entomology and
ornithology, his father's manuscripts suffered the same fate. At
any rate, there is no clue to a very large collection of papers,
supposed to have fallen into Mr. T. C. Heysham's hands. The
history of entomology would have been largely benefited had the
Doctor and his son's researches found their way into the world.

CHAPTER VI.

HIS PERSONALITY, HABITS, AND CHARACTER, PATRIOTIC AND SOCIAL—HIS
MEDICAL CONTEMPORARIES AND CLERICAL FRIENDS—THE MUSIC OF
NATURE—MEDICAL ZEAL—MAGISTERIAL LABOURS—HIS DEATH.

DR. HEYSHAM was one of the most handsome men of the
Border City. He was tall, and well-proportioned in every way,
and his gait was that of a man of business and energy. His
dress was no less conspicuous than his person. He wore a blue
coat, with bright buttons, a light-coloured vest, buff or nankeen
breeches, and large top-boots. When he was a young man the
fashion was to have very long hair, and such was the profusion
of his brown locks in early life that they almost reached his
knees. As the mode changed, the hair was drawn up and
combed backwards in a curious way. After a time the wig came
into vogue, with its white powder and horrid "pig-tail." The
latter, or queue, he wore in full proportion till 1820, and then
adopted a somewhat modified form, which he continued till the
day of his death. He lived long enough to see all the styles of
artificiality done away with, and the natural hair restored to man,

who had, in this and other directions, been so long the victim of fashion and absurdity.

In a water-coloured drawing of Heysham, taken in early manhood, you see a fine open countenance marked by intelli-gence and earnestness, regular features, blue eyes, full-sized nose and chin, and a mouth as graceful in outline as any woman's. The artist, wishing to make the accessories of the portrait sub-servient to the sentiment of the man, placed Heysham by a table, upon which stood a falcon of his own shooting, and in his hand a flower, as illustrative of the doctor's botanical and zoological studies.

The lithographed portrait on the frontispiece of this volume is taken from a miniature of Dr. Heysham in his sixty-sixth year, and acknowledged to be a perfect likeness. A bust was also made of him in his seventy-second year, by the famed sculptor, Musgrave Lewthwaite Watson. Both works show a lofty, broad, and finely-proportioned head, with comparatively small occipital region. The ear is well lobed, the nose aquiline and notable. The mouth and chin show no alteration from their pristine regularity and character even at the age of seventy-two years.

Dr. Heysham professed a strong *physique*, and was capable of great and long-continued exertions. He was an early riser, and almost invariably the first person to survey from the west walls of the city the picturesque views of the Vale of Cauda, and to judge of the weather indications from the grey dawn. He was often abroad for three hours before breakfast, botanising, or, it may be said, naturalising, as nothing in animated nature escaped his attention. He was one of the hard-headed philosophic sort of men, and strongly-stomached, like his friend Dr. Paley, the eminent divine ; but the doctor of divinity was not a match for the doctor of medicine in the hours of alcoholic enjoyment. Heysham used to say that he had no illness through life, and that his stomach was a pleasure and delight to him, so that probably he endorsed neighbour Paley's oft-expressed opinion of the stomach being "a lazy organ, and always better of something to do." He never had toothache, and never used tooth-powder ; but washed his mouth daily with warm water. His teeth were rather dark-coloured, with the exception of one, said to be a canine tooth, that he got very late in life, and which shone like a pearl in the midst of the " old set."

His mode of living was somewhat peculiar. He rose at five o'clock, and drank a large tumbler of cold water fresh drawn from the well. Woe betide his maid if she attempted to impose the previous night's supply of water upon his palate ! He then walked out to enjoy " the incense-breathing morn " by the river side, and onwards to Kingmoor, where he had a farm. He breakfasted between nine and ten o'clock. A bowl containing a quart of the morning's new milk, with its cream, a second bowl, containing two raw eggs, and a jug of boiling water, formed the breakfast display. He poured the boiling water on the eggs, stirred them well together, and swallowed them; the milk followed, and the breakfast was speedily over. He took no bread to his morning's meal, unless he had a supply of West-moreland oat-cake, which he was in the habit of spreading with butter thicker than the cake itself, and adding a great quantity of salt to it. He dined at two o'clock *en famille*, and made a good hearty meal, and drank a few glasses of wine. He had no tea, excepting once a year at a lady friend's house. His supper at nine o'clock, which he took alone, was a heavy meal of animal food — beefsteaks, game, or welsh rabbits, etc. Occasionally he would eat half-a-pound of nuts; but whatever he took in the way of solids a "stiff glass of rum-punch" followed. No Carlisle citizen went to bed with so good a "night-cap" as the doctor's rum-punch. He was as fond of sweetmeats as any schoolboy to the last day of his life. He snuffed immoderately, as his frilled shirt testified but too strongly to all men.

He was naturally reserved in manner, and this trait was the more noted by his family at home, when they knew that his feelings were acute and his affections warm for his children. Like the *paterfamilias* of that day, he was rigid and exacting of the performance of school and domestic duties, and did his best to cultivate the home virtues. When he threw off his reserve, and

II

entered upon the discussion of natural history, his talk was
animated ; and his description, whether of birds or scenery, or
the narrative of his excursions in search of his favourite pursuits,
was deeply engrossing to his hearers.   In his public relations he
was far from being retired, for there he showed earnestness of purpose, and no small share of determined will in upholding what he
believed to be the right.   He took an active part in all matters
affecting the social, commercial, and political life of Carlisle.

Though busy in his medical capacity, and for long the chief
physician or rather medical practitioner of the city, he entered
with practical zest upon the business concerns affecting the city's
welfare.   In some departments of Carlisle commerce he was not
only a willing coadjutor, but an active leader.   He established a
cotton-spinning mill about 1800, and directed, for a time at least,
an iron foundry ; in various ways he endeavoured to promote the
spirit of enterprise, as well among the denizens of Carlisle as
among the richer families in the neighbourhood.   He had an eye
for business and money-making, and lost no opportunity of
advancing his material interests.

When Dr. Heysham settled in Carlisle, the political interests
of the borough were being usurped by the Tory Lowthers, to
whose sleeves he seems unhesitatingly to have attached himself.
The bait was tempting ; all the magisterial and other appoint-
ments in Cumberland were very much in the hands of the Low-

thers, and these " baubles of office," the perquisites of political
subserviency to so many " Shallows " and " Slenders " in Cumberland (alas ! of such Justices " the cry is still they come !")
influenced the decision of men seeking place and public distinction. His partisanship was pretty well evidenced in 1816, when
he and the Rev. Dr. Lowry permitted a felon to come out of
Carlisle Jail to give his vote in favour of a Lowther candidate
against the renowned Whig, John Christian Curwen. Towards his
latter days, Dr. Heysham, contrary to the wonted rule affecting
change of political opinion, leant towards the Spencer and Russell
party in the State, and the last vote he gave at a Carlisle
election was in favour of the Reform candidates.

His patriotic feeling was keen, and oft assumed a highly
demonstrative form, especially during the war with France.
When news of import were expected, no one manifested more
eagerness to know the tide of affairs than Heysham, whose im-
patience led him to mount his pony, and to ride three or four
miles on the South road, to meet the London mail, which he
stopped; and on getting his information returned in full gallop to
the city. Brimful of news, he sought the mayor's house, and
thundered most lustily with the knocker, so as to make his
Worship alive to the situation of the hour. One of his gallops
up Botchergate was ominously looked upon as a hasty retreat
to the city, and drew crowds of citizens after him, curious to

know if Bonaparte had crossed Barrock Fell, and if Carlisle was to surrender without a blow. He was the first to announce the proclamation of peace in 1814, and this he did in a manner to be heard by the men and women of " Merrie Carlisle." " Peace, peace, glorious peace !" he cried along his route through the southern suburb, whilst he kept urging his pony to its utmost speed to reach the Town Hall and the mayor's residence. He was deeply affected by national events. Disasters, and loss of human life on the battle-fields of Europe, caused him to shed tears ; on the other hand, peace and British prestige made him as buoyant and enthusiastically joyous as the liveliest youth. He was dining with his friends the Mounseys of Castletown when the news of Waterloo arrived. He read aloud the whole story of the victory to the assembled guests, and as he read he cried and sobbed throughout.

Dr. Heysham greatly treasured the company of his friends, and seldom failed in his loquacity to give currency to his opinions, if not to impress them upon the social circles of Carlisle. Medical men naturally possess advantages in society; their education, if worthy of their calling, should fit them for the discussion of special as well as general subjects of conversational interest ; they mix with all ranks and gradations of men, and thereby possess the opportunity of knowing the feelings and wishes of a local community ; and should they be gifted with tolerable judgment and facility of talk, they are capable of exercising a toward and pleasant influence among their neighbours. Heysham ranked with the intel- lectual folk, and these formed but a small party in the Carlisle district. He was a frequent guest at the deanery and prebendal houses within the precincts of the Abbey, when these institutions were presided over by men of notable excellence, like Dean Percy, the Prebendaries Law, and Archdeacon Paley. Nor was he less esteemed by the neighbouring squirearchy, the first Sir James Graham, Bart. of Netherby, and his more noted son, the States- man of Victoria's reign, the excellent Henry Howard of Corby Castle, the Loshes of Woodside, and other county families. Now, the doctor liked a good dinner, and its grateful accom- paniments of good wine, and both were most liberally served to the visitors of Corby Castle and Woodside. In his professional rounds he did not lose sight of the hospitality of his friends and the well-furnished mahogany.

Of his medical contemporaries in Carlisle, mention need only be made of Dr. Thomas Blamire, an esteemed practitioner and high Tory, who, in his latter days, filled the civic chair no less than six times ; Dr. Robert Harrington, an eccentric gentleman, who wrote a curious book on chemistry, in which the "phlogiston," if not the alchemy, of the past was made to play a part in the settlement of new and doubtful doctrines ; and Sir Joseph Dacre Appleby Gilpin, an army-surgeon, whose valuable services in

America and the West Indies had obtained him the distinction of
knighthood, and who returned to his native city in 1806, to enjoy
his honours and the high esteem of his fellow citizens, who named
him four times to the mayoralty.   His knowledge of the world,
his medical experience, courteous disposition, and urbanity, made
Sir Joseph a great acquisition to Carlisle.   Four such medical
worthies as Blamire, Harrington, Gilpin, and Heysham, could
hardly be met with in a provincial town.   All of them died at an
advanced age, and close upon each other; Sir Joseph Gilpin in his
ninetieth year, and Heysham in his eighty-first year, died within
a few months of each other.

The cultivation of letters, of poesy, general history, and
archæology, was pretty nearly confined to the cathedral precincts,
with the notable exception of Miss Susanna Blamire, of the Oaks
and Thackwood, who spent several winters in Carlisle, and died
(1795) within its walls.   Reared under happy circumstances, she
early displayed a poetic faculty, a love of music, and a greater
love of fun.   Her poesy has become historical, as it fairly merited ;
and with her name has been appropriately attached the ennobling
epithet of the "Muse of Cumberland."   She was as bright as
Nature in her summer mood, and as bonny as the bonniest of
Cumbria's fair daughters.   So sunny and kind and graceful a
person should have bloomed under more favourable skies ; in her
position, however, she was ever joyful, and not less the cause of

pleasant mirth to others. Her songs, "What ails this heart of mine?" "And ye shall walk in silk attire," and numerous effusions of local interest, will live for ever in the ballad literature of the North Country.

Edmund Law held rule at Rose Castle as Bishop of Carlisle from 1767 to 1787. Eminent in theology and metaphysics, the biographer of John Locke, with whose philosophic principles he was deeply imbued, and the attached friend of Archdeacon Paley, Bishop Law will ever hold a worthy place in English history. He was succeeded by Dr. John Douglas, a Scotchman, who discoursed on "Miracles," and had a reputation in the literary world of Dr. Samuel Johnson and his contemporaries. In the year 1778, that marked Heysham's settling in Carlisle, Thomas Percy, the son of a small grocer at Bridgenorth, who had proved himself a scholar of high repute in peculiar paths of historic lore, was made Dean of Carlisle. The author of *Reliques of Ancient English Poetry,* and other works of undoubted interest, was on pleasant terms with Heysham till he was appointed to the see of Dromore. It was fortunate, nay, highly opportune, for the doctor to become a denizen of Carlisle on the advent of Dean Percy, and to secure the friendship and co-operation of so influential a divine in his schemes of medical philanthropy for the benefit of the poor and the general welfare of the inhabitants at large. He was more aided by Isaac Milner, who was brought up as a Leeds weaver,

and worked at his loom with a copy of *Tacitus* at his side, who,
from the humble rank of sizar, rose to the presidency of his
College, after attaining the proud position of senior wrangler
and *Incomparabilis* at Cambridge. He succeeded Jeffrey
Ekins at the Deanery of Carlisle. Dean Milner discharged his
social duties with fitting grace, and his clerical labours with
dignity and power. Holding prebendal stalls at this time were
John and George Law, the sons of Bishop Law, who also shone as
scholars, philanthropists, and preachers. Greater than these just
named, and greater than all men in his own line of thought, and not
improbably of his epoch, was William Paley, who, as prebendary,
archdeacon, and chancellor, was closely related to Carlisle from 1780
till 1795. Joseph Dacre Carlyle, the son of a Carlisle physician,
succeeded Dr. Paley. Eminent as an Arabic scholar, and among
the first of oriental travellers, he explored the valuable libraries
of Mount Athos, and other book-treasures of the East, and meri-
toriously earned a high name among men of letters. Professor
Carlyle lived in a retired way, and was looked upon by the illiter-
ate of the city as a kind of " human curiosity," from having been
to the Holy Sepulchre of Jerusalem ! The Rev. R. Markham,*

---

* It was Prebendary Markham who, in 1804, gave orders to get the fine
capitals of the Gothic columns in the Cathedral cleaned from plaster and white-
wash, which had been accumulating for centuries, so as totally to obscure " the
beautiful ornaments which, when freed from the rubbish that surrounded them,

son of the Archbishop of York, and prebendary of Carlisle Cathedral, was also one of Heysham's friends.

Bishop Law and his sons, who afterwards rose to lawn sleeves,
Dean Percy, Archdeacon Paley, Dr. Carlyle, and Dean Milner, were
all associated with the cathedral interests of Carlisle within the
limited period of seventeen years. Such an array of worthy
historical names could hardly be found in any single episcopate
since the days of the Reformation. Heysham, it may be presumed,
prized his good fortune in enjoying the private friendship of men
so distinguished ; whilst, in his public efforts, to have them as
coadjutors was half-way to a successful attainment of his wishes.
After the days of Dean Milner there was, more or less,
falling off in the city's episcopate. Dean Hodgson was more a
Cockney fashionable and courtier, than a divine ; and though
men of classical repute succeeded him, they took no real part in
educational work, they added not a line to history or science,
philology or *belles lettres*, and above all, advanced not their own
theological interests by that faintest of religious lights, the local
sermon, " published by request."

There is reason for believing that Dr. Heysham occasionally
aided Dr. Paley in his anatomical and natural history inquiries,
upon which to found his *Natural Theology*, a work commenced on

discovered some of the finest *alto-relievos* that ever came from the workman's
chisel."

the banks of the Cauda at Dalston, and completed at Bishop-
Wearmouth. One proof may be instanced, as it is established in
the writer's mind beyond all doubt. Paley and Heysham were
dining with Prebendary Law in the Abbey, when the conversation
fell upon natural history. Heysham spoke of the peculiar
arrangement and attachment of the minute portions of the goose's
feather. Paley's curiosity was excited, a feather was got, and
upon it Heysham demonstrated the facts as they are recorded in
the *Natural Theology*, published some years subsequently. Yet
Paley, as if forgetful of the source from whence he really obtained
it, credits a French writer with the description. This is the more
remarkable that he seldom quoted anybody's authority for any of
his statements, whilst here he omitted the nice opportunity of
doing justice to an old friend and Carlisle associate.

Dr. Heysham got the credit of being *facile princeps*, if not the
founder, of a very jovial party, consisting of about a dozen gentlemen, who dined at each other's houses during the winter months ;
for the laudable purpose, it is presumed, of lessening the dispirit-
ing influence of fogs and gloom, and of driving all dull care away.
And if rich viands and strong vintages could fire the " patriotic
bosom," Heysham and his select circle must have been among the
noblest of Britons. To get up a good appetite, the Jovials dined
at three o'clock, then held to be an extremely late hour by the
higher classes of Carlisle ; they rose from table about ten at night,

during which time "mine host" and each guest put three bottles of strong port below his belt! On rare occasions, such as a victory by Nelson or the dashing Cochrane, the fourth bottle to each man was held to be the right mode of rendering the fact historical! Whether three or four bottles were the order of the day, Dr. Heysham went home to sup off his favourite nuts, and to give the last strong fillip to his stomach by a hearty draught of hot rum punch.*

It may have been that Heysham's companions, the majority of whom were classically educated, wished to imitate the Roman youths who, according to Martial, in drinking the health of their sweethearts, used to quaff as many cups as there were letters in the fair one's name—

> " Nævia sex cyathis, septem Justina bibatur,
> Quinque Lycas, Lyde quatuor, Ida tribus,
> Omnis ab infuso numeratur amica Falerno."

And with short names, *Lyde* and *Ida*, there could be no difficulty in the young Roman proving his gallantry ; far otherwise would it be to-day with the Henriettas and Josephines, demanding

---

* The "three-bottle men" of Carlisle seem to have borrowed their principles from the famous Avicenna, the Arabian physician, who recommended it as an excellent thing for the health to get completely drunk once a month. In Cumberland, within the last twenty-five years, the writer has met with "old hands" at the bottle, who could cite popular authorities in medicine for a regular debauch ; and the pious Hannah More has been quoted in support of this mode of doing in preference to regular habits of moderate drinking.

ten or more libations of their loving votaries. But the Roman could not cope with the descendants of the ancient Briton, when you call to mind, that instead of the mild Falernian, our Cumberland topers quaffed about thirty glasses of strong port at one sitting, and afterwards found their way home, even to a distance in the country. These were not the men to drink small beer. Heysham had no faith in the *Cerevisia tenuis* of his medical cloth ; even the *Cerevisia potentior,* " Old October," was of little esteem compared with strong port. What marvellous constitutions these men must have had ! All lived to a great age, and enjoyed life to the very last.*

* Upwards of twenty-five years ago the writer of these pages had the benefit of listening to his old friend, Mr. Thomas Mounsey of Carlisle, recounting incidents in the lives and doings of the " *Three-bottle Men,*" of which he was a junior member. Among the conspicuous of the symposial brethren worthy of high rank in " the Heysham set " were—

1. Mr. Thomas Ramshay of Naworth, characterised as a " jolly fellow," a shrewd, hard-headed, massive Cumbrian, as ever sat under the shadows of Brampton Moat.

2. The Rev. Samuel Bateman of Newbiggin Hall, originally rector of Hardingstone, in Northamptonshire, but who, on his marriage with the co-heiress of the Aglionby family, forsook Mother Church and became a country squire, and a prominent member of the Carlisle Hunt. Bucolic interests were viewed by him as pillars of the British Constitution, and sports and pastimes as the *beau ideal* of life. He kept dogs for all sorts of game, in Cumberland, and hunted with his pack of beagles to the very last hour, and actually died on the field of his glory. He wore a three-cocked hat, green coat and bright buttons (sometimes hid under a spencer), white shorts, and huge top-boots, and

Dr. Heysham had no ear for music, and could not distinguish "Rule Britannia" from "God save the Queen;" yet he knew the notes of every bird in Cumberland. Thus he seemed to verify that—

> "The birds instructed man,
> And taught him music ere his art began."

The natural or living notes alone impressed his auditory nerve, or rather the *sensorium*, and these notes could be isolated as well

over his shoulder swung the bugle-horn, with its tassels and pendants—the veritable " Parson Samuel " of the good old times !

3. Thomas Benson, a Carlisle gentleman (a steady Whig whose father had been confidential agent of the Duke of Portland), held to be reserved, if not sedate, in general society, but who, being placed under the influence of the normal quantity of "three bottles," found his facial muscles relaxed and his tongue pretty garrulous.

4. William Dacre of Kirklinton, better known as " Squire Dacre," or " Billy Dacre," was " a jolly old cock " at all times and seasons of life. Springing from the loins, direct or indirect, of the great Dacres of the north, but caring more for strong drinks than noble lineage, he got the credit of being the first at a feast and the last at a fray. He attended all funerals, and pretty generally got drunk at them. On one occasion the mourning neighbours, under Squire Dacre's example, got so oblivious that they reached the place of interment without the coffin ! All country funerals in those days, it should be stated, were marked by eating and excessive drinking, and sad stories could be told of the prevailing customs.

5. Joseph Liddell of Moorhouse was a lawyer, and presided over all commissions of bankruptcy in and about Carlisle, whereon he showed the " eyes severe " and the rigid features of judicial wisdom. Among his neighbours he was held to be " cantankerous," but at the symposial gatherings of the district he showed himself fit company for the most convivial of his countrymen.

as remembered, whilst the tones elicited from musical instru-
ments sounded like a jumble.   His instance presented an incon-
gruity of no ordinary kind.   In common parlance it might be
said he was musical to nature, but not to art.   He readily dis-
criminated, nay enjoyed and thoroughly remembered, the notes of
birds, but could make nothing of the artificial or instrumental
sounds.   He seemed alive to melody, or the pleasure arising from
the succession of simple sounds, as the notes or call of birds ;
but dull, nay, altogether incomprehensive, to that agreement of
component vibrations in simple sounds which constitutes them
musical.   His case proves that the music in nature is beyond all
reduction to the pianoforte.   He loved the " chime of earliest birds"
as much as Milton's Eve ; and no denizen of the crowded throng
belonging to pent-up cities, could more fully realise the enjoyment
depicted by Virgil of listening whilst

 " Small birds with chiming and with chirping changed their song."*

As a medical man, Dr. Heysham is said to have enjoyed a
large share of what is called " public confidence," yet he never
made more than £400 a-year by practice among the best families.
He was hardly the person to become " a fashionable doctor," and

---

* A lady, long known to the writer, who has gradually become deaf after
middle life, and cannot hear the voice of her friends unless it be raised exceedingly
high, can nevertheless detect the faintest note of the piano nearly as well as
when her hearing was quite perfect.

it is doubtful, as his income tends to show, if his engagements
lay much among the middle classes of Carlisle. He did not
neglect the advance of his art; he was, in one sense, always a
student, ready to take advantage of the new lights brought to
bear upon the field of science and discovery. Thus he very
early recognised the great import of Dr. Jenner's notable observations, that persons who had become affected by "cowpox" inoculation on the dairy farms in the south, either escaped "smallpox"
altogether, or had the disease in a greatly modified form. He
proved his trust in this, one of the greatest discoveries ever vouch-
safed to the followers of physic, by vaccinating his youngest
daughter, Isabella, on the 23d October 1800, when she was
scarcely a month old. For a good and obvious purpose he made
this fact publicly known in Cumberland, and people listened to
his commendations the more eagerly, that the physician had
experimented upon his own child, and with entire success. He
was the first to introduce vaccination to Carlisle, if not the north-
western district of England—at a time, too, when the practice
stood in a more or less doubtful position both in London and the
provinces. As he joined heartily in the homage paid to Dr.
Jenner, so he continued through life to urge the use of vaccination as an almost infallible* preventive of the worst forms of

---

* In the same year (1800) that Dr. Blamire vaccinated Dr. Heysham's
daughter, another child was vaccinated, who, nevertheless, took smallpox in the

smallpox. Lady Mary Montagu had done much, by the introduction of inoculation or natural pox, to lessen the virulence of
the disease. Jenner came to sweep it altogether away. And
had the opinions expressed in 1869, or thereabouts, by the late
Sir J. Y. Simpson, the greatest physician of our day, been acted
upon, there is no doubt the disease would have been stamped out
from the British Isles, and for ever. In proof of this, look to
Ireland, where compulsory vaccination exists ; only one death from
smallpox is reported as occurring in the whole of that country
during the quarter ending June 1870.

The dangers of medical practice were considerable a century
ago, especially among a closely-packed urban population : even
Carlisle was far from being exempt from such contingencies as
the development and spread of jail-fever proved. Ignorant folk
would set all natural laws at defiance. When the sick man
needed fresh air and cold water, they closed both doors and
windows, enveloped him in blankets, and obstinately refused his
cry for cooling liquids. Heysham's pathological perception led
him to insist on his patients obeying the instincts of nature for
cooling hygienic measures — a service of kindness that should

natural way in 1808. This case of smallpox occurring after vaccination was
the first failure of protection that had been observed in England ; and Dr.
Heysham noted the fact in a letter to Dr. Jenner. The " pock-mark " from
vaccination on the arm of the boy at the time he was seized with smallpox left
no room for cavil on the subject.

have earned for him the gratitude of his fellow-citizens. Most of his contemporaries suffered from attacks of fever caught in the abodes of the dirty poor ; but Heysham, who could walk or ride all day, drink his wine at dinner, and punch at bed-time, and sleep with a single sheet of covering upon his person in the cold months, was able to resist the casualties attending his calling, and to pass unscathed to his eightieth year.

Like others of his cloth, he had his medical squabbles, and, like the rest of the busy members of the community, his bothers and legal differences,* all which he met with a determined hand. He founded the Dispensary, and was equally ready to aid his friend, Mr. Robert Mounsey of Castletown, who originated the establishment of a House of Recovery, or Fever-House,† that came to be built on a portion of Heysham's property. He promoted the town's improvements, the paving and lighting of the streets ; and formation of the canal connecting Carlisle with the Solway Firth at Bowness. In short, he helped every work calculated to

---

* His litigation with the Corporation about some property at Kingmoor called forth the powers of a young barrister, who, in the absence of a leading counsel, got Heysham's brief. This was Mr. Law, fourth son of Bishop Law, who sat up all night to master his first case, and won it next day with great éclat. He was at once brought into notice, and, in time, led the Northern Circuit, and became the famous Lord Ellenborough.

† With the extension of the railways to Carlisle, this "House" became untenable, as one for "Recovery of the Sick ;" therefore a new Fever Hospital was established at Crozier Lodge, near the Cumberland Infirmary.

I

benefit the citizens at large. His purchases of land and other business avocations turned out well, and the public companies (excepting the canal) in which he took a leading part, owed something of their success to his energetic support and sagacity.

He had his holidays in naturalising and shooting, and twice a-year his greyhound coursing with "Parson Bateman" of Newbiggin Hall, and Mr. Ramshay on the Naworth Castle property.

Dr. Heysham was a magistrate and deputy-lieutenant of the counties of Cumberland and Westmoreland. Though the most active and useful of men in Carlisle, he never occupied its civic chair. His medical contemporaries, Sir Joseph Gilpin and Dr. Blamire, frequently obtained the distinction. As a Tory and friend of the Lowthers, who had the Carlisle corporation of that day in their hands, Heysham might have expected the mayoralty thrust upon him; probably the fact of his having a will of his own, was held objectionable in a court ruled by fogyism and Lowtherism alike. In his magisterial capacity he sat along with the Rev. Dr. Grisdale, and afterwards with the Rev. Dr. Thomas Lowry, at the Globe Inn, Scotch Street, Carlisle, on the market-days, to administer justice to the citizens and offending lieges. There were two rival judicial institutions or boards of magistrates holding court in Carlisle. The mayor, aided or not by an ex-mayor, sat in the Town Hall, and his jurisdiction was probably limited to the city itself. Drs. Heysham, Grisdale, and Lowry, apparently took cognisance of both town and country interests. The dual system was a bad one for the suitors of justice, inas- much as it opened two doors to the contentious and brawling citizens, and thereby fostered a great amount of needless litigation. The magistrates and their clerks were of course partial to the con- tinuance of a mode which brought grist to their mills ; in other words, filled their pockets at the expense of the poorer lieges. An example of the justices' justice of 1830 may be given. A and B quarrel, and both " will go to law." A gets Dr. Heysham to issue a summons against B, and B does the same by A on the consent of the mayor. The parties, A and B, appear before Heysham and his colleague, sitting in the parlour of a common public-house, thronged with farmers and country bumpkins drinking beer. The writer is describing what he himself saw as a boy. Justices Heysham and Lowry occupied arm-chairs by the side of the fire ; Mr. T. C. Heysham officiated as clerk. A table, covered with green baize, stood in the centre of the room, and upon it a good sized blue basin. The litigants attempted to state their grievances, when the clerk, anticipating a long palaver, interrupted them, and explained the nature of the case to the " Ancients " of the court, and then addressed the complainants thus, " Now, A and B, why do you quarrel ? you are neighbours, and should not have domestic rows in the street ; try and keep the peace, or we'll make you." When a pause occurred, Dr. Heysham uttered in a loud voice the words, " Pay, pay," meaning the costs of the summoning, and Parson Lowry was nothing loth in emphasizing the pecuniary sentiment of his colleague. A and B, seeing they could make no better of it, fumbled out of their pockets the demands of the court and clerk's fees, and paid them down. As they left the justices' parlour, the old cry of " Pay, pay," mingled in their ears with the sounds of the silver dropped into the blue basin. When the majesty of the law had been maintained, and the business of the day was over, the spoils of the blue basin were divided between the acting officials; then the doctors of divinity and physic called for a glass of brandy-punch, over which they refreshed their jaded minds, and not without some hearty chuckles at the follies of the age, and the weakness of their victims. Heysham afterwards dined off a beefsteak-pie ; and in this, as in other matters, he showed his methodical turn by cutting a piece of paper of the exact size he wished the pie to be made, for the guidance of the landlady of the Globe, whose culinary accuracy was tested by both paper and pie being presented together at table.

" The Blue Basin " was the subject of many a joke against Dr. Heysham and his colleague. A very unexpected claimant for part of the contents of the said basin appeared one market-day. A tax-gatherer, who could not, after repeated calls at Crosby, get Dr. Lowry to pay his dues, walked into the justices' sanctuary at Carlisle, and helped himself out of the basin to the extent of the taxes due him by the clerical defaulter. Both the presiding genii called out lustily against such an unheard-of intrusion upon the sacred domain of one of his Majesty's courts of justice, but the tax-collector held by his dues and the interests of the national Exchequer.

With advancing years, Dr. Heysham, like too many in their senility, got fond of money and the means that enriched. When individuals came before him as a magistrate, to take affidavits as to the validity of documents, and had to pay him a shilling for administering the oath, he used to make sure of the genuineness of the silver coin, by saying to the person, " You swear to the truth of the contents of this paper, and" then pointing to the fee on the table, " that this shilling is good."

His " Seventies" found him a hale old man, with all his faculties intact, but before the approach of the eightieth year his walking powers were visibly enfeebled. A very gradually developed paralysis of the motory actions of the body set in ; his gait became shuffling and slow ; other parts of his system also betrayed more or less decadence. Still he clung to the sweets of office, and would discharge the duties of his magisterial position to the very last day of his life. He was unable to go to the Globe Inn on Saturday the 22d of March 1834, but, in his own house, Dr. Lowry and he transacted magisterial business. He saw his medical man the same night, supped heartily, and took two glasses of rum-punch, and seemed tolerably comfortable. Next morning, Sunday, Dr. Heysham was found moribund, and before noon passed away in his eighty-first year.

His remains were interred in the burial-ground of St. Mary's, and in the most private manner. In the new Carlisle cemetery has been erected a small pyramid of granite, upon which are inscribed his birth and death, also that of his wife and their deceased sons and daughters. A few years ago Miss Heysham placed a beautiful memorial window in the eastern termination of one of the side aisles of the cathedral, to commemorate her father's character and virtues. The writer would humbly suggest that the admirable bust of Dr. Heysham, done by Mr. Watson the sculptor, and now in the possession of the Rev. John Heysham, the Vicar of Lazonby, should find a place in the Town Hall, or Courts of Justice of Carlisle, that future generations may see the image of a man who contributed largely to the material interests of the city, and by his Bills of Mortality made Carlisle known to the rest of the civilized world.

CHAPTER VII.

REVIEW OF DR. HEYSHAM'S LABOURS; THEIR APPLICATION TO LIFE INSUR-
ANCE—" THE CARLISLE TABLE" COMPARED WITH "THE ENGLISH
TABLES"—ESTIMATE FORMED OF DR. HEYSHAM'S SERVICES AT HOME
AND ABROAD.

DR. HEYSHAM was a man of broad and vigorous thought, highly discriminative, and sagacious. He belonged to a class of minds that may be characterised as eliminating and suggestive; his readiness in separating the corn from the chaff, and in clearing the ground for correct deductions, was only equalled by his ability to apply patent data to the elucidation of unknown laws. Zealous and painstaking in the solution of all questions submitted to his notice, and an adept at figures and classification, he was well suited to the numerical methods of inquiry, and to achieve success in a field but little trodden—that of Vital Statistics.

Bills of Mortality had engaged other minds than his both at home and abroad, and previous to his time; but no one in England seems to have bestowed the same care in collecting the facts, and notifying the circumstances that necessarily creep in and modify the construction of all formulas resting on the contingencies of life and death. Slovenliness and incorrectness had attended

most inquiries pertaining to health and longevity, and done no
small amount of harm ; thus the British Government, as will be
noted presently, trusting to exaggerated rates of mortality, had
unwittingly robbed the national Exchequer, by their grants of
annuities and pensions based on false data.

Dr. Heysham first made sure of the number of the population
of Carlisle by a method that, in point of accuracy, almost amounted
to a personal registration of each individual family.   In collating
the death-rolls, he recognised the age, sex, and matrimonial relations in the registered forms ; nor did he overlook the general
questions—the national status, the influence of war and peace, the
dearth or abundance of provisions, the state of trade and local
interests, the seasons of the year, the meteorological phenomena
of the district, the prevalence of epidemics, and all other circumstances bearing upon the health, sickness, and mortality of the city.
He kept his eye upon the actual increase of births beyond mere
baptismal records; he noted the flow and ebb of Scottish and Irish
immigration ; the number whose patriotism led them to join the
army and navy ; and all the fluctuating circumstances surrounding
an urban population.

The accuracy which guided Heysham's observations on the rate
of mortality in Carlisle proved of the highest significance to the
general community of Britain, and, it may be added, to the world at
large.   Wherever the question of life assurance has been discussed
throughout the civilized globe, Heysham's labours have been recog-

nised and extolled for their meritorious application and usefulness. For it need hardly be said that the Life or Mortality Table is the basis upon which the whole science of life assurance rests ; it is essential to the vital statistician as the barometer is to the meteorologist, the balance to the physicist, and the test-tube to the chemist.

The value of Dr. Heysham's work in Carlisle can be best instanced by the serious errors that sprang from incorrect observation and records made elsewhere. When Dr. Price was constructing the Northampton tables, a great number of Baptists lived in the town who did not sanction infant baptism, and thereby reducing the ratio of the christenings to the births, led Dr. Price to believe that the population of Northampton was stationary ! The average lifetime in Northampton was in reality about 30 years, but Dr. Price, overlooking the Baptists, assumed it to be only 24. It is *now* 37½, or 13 years (*one-third*) more than he took it to be ! " And as a curious confirmation of the error, the mortality of the Equitable Society (which first used the Northampton Table) was *one-third less than that Table predicted.* But the most serious part of the business remains yet to be told. The Government adopted these tables as the basis for its annuity schemes. The same error which gave the Equitable and other societies using the Table *one-third too much premium,* induced the Government to grant annuities by *one-third too large* for the price charged ; and before the error was rectified, about two millions of money were lost to the country by these annuity transactions."

Guided by Dr. Heysham's published observations, and the explanations elicited by his lengthened correspondence (set forth for the first time in the appendix to this volume) with the author of the Bills of Mortality, Mr. Joshua Milne constructed his famed " Carlisle Table." From the date of the publication of Mr. Milne's table in 1816, a new era in the life assurance world sprang up. Conjecture, occasionally wild if not chaotic, had to give way to a healthful reasoning upon legitimate data and sober facts.

Mr. Milne, whose experience as actuary to the Sun Life Assurance Society and high sagacity entitled his considerations to the fullest attention, was of opinion, that although the Carlisle Table had been constructed from the mortality of two parishes only, the results it exhibited would probably vary very little "from the general law that obtains throughout the kingdom, taking town and country together, if we except the children under five years of age, or at most under ten." "In other respects," says the editor of the *Insurance Guide,* " it has undoubtedly been the best guide to healthy life" in England, from the date of its publication at least up to the completion of Dr. Farr's tables. It gave the expectation of life for males at 30 in Carlisle at $34\frac{1}{4}$ years. The average duration throughout England at the same age is $33\frac{3}{4}$ years ; and in Sweden and Finland, $32\frac{3}{4}$." Though the table showed results slightly too favourable for the whole country at all ages, the great fact remains, " that all properly conducted offices, based upon the Carlisle Table, have met their engagements, and for the most part had very large surpluses to spare."

Benjamin Gompertz, F.R.S., in his calculations by logarithmic formulas* of the value of life at certain ages, shows the striking accuracy of Milne's tables formed on the Carlisle Bills of Mortality. Thus he found the value of the joint lives for ages from 20 to 30, at 3 per cent and Carlisle mortality, to be 16·745, which, according to Milne's tables, should be 16·749 ; an " insignificant difference," as Gompertz very truly observes.

It is a matter of fact, that the Carlisle Table, founded by Joshua Milne on the Carlisle Bills of Mortality, is used by a majority of the existing insurance offices. "The English Tables" based on 30 years' observation, and on data obtained from the records of mortality over the whole kingdom, will probably receive the attention of offices now forming, yet the two tables differ comparatively little ; as is evidenced on the following pages 124 and 125. The Carlisle shows the lightest mortality, except at the extreme ages, namely from 0 to 5 years, and from 74 years down to the end of the Table, with the exception of one or two years. The minimum mortality in the Carlisle Tables occurs at the age of 10 ; in the English Table at 12.

---

* "On the Nature of the Functions expressive of the Laws of Human Mortality, and on a New Mode of Determining the Value of Life Contingencies :" in a letter to Francis Baily, F.R.S. ; by Benjamin Gompertz, F.R.S. (*Lond. Philos. Trans.*, vol. cxv. p. 513). Gompertz had previously written on the same subject (*loc. cit.* A.D. 1820).

ENGLISH LIFE TABLE No. 1. MALE AND FEMALE.

Age.	Number who complete that year.	Number who died during the next year.
53	4434	76
54	4358	78
55	4279	84
56	4194	90
57	4103	96
58	4007	101
59	3906	106
60	3799	112
61	3687	117
62	3569	123
63	3446	128
64	3318	133
65	3185	138
66	3046	142
67	2904	147
68	2759	150
69	2606	153
70	2453	156
71	2297	157
72	2139	158
73	1981	158
74	1823	156

CARLISLE TABLE. MALE AND FEMALE.

Age.	Number who complete that year.	Number who died during the next year.
53	4211	68
54	4143	70
55	4070	73
56	4000	76
57	3924	82
58	3842	93
59	3749	106
60	3643	122
61	3521	126
62	3395	127
63	3268	125
64	3143	125
65	3018	124
66	2894	123
67	2771	123
68	2648	124
69	2525	124
70	2401	134
71	2277	146
72	2143	156
73	1997	166
74	1841	

ENGLISH LIFE TABLE No. 1. MALE AND FEMALE.

Age.	Number who complete that year.	Number who died during the next year.
0	10,000	1463
1	8,536	526
2	8,010	271
3	7,739	185
4	7,553	133
5	7,420	104
6	7,315	83
7	7,232	67
8	7,164	56
9	7,108	46
10	7,061	39
11	7,022	36
12	6,985	35
13	6,950	41
14	6,909	46
15	6,862	49
16	6,813	50
17	6,762	51
18	6,710	52
19	6,658	52
20	6,605	53
21	6,552	54

CARLISLE TABLE. MALE AND FEMALE.

Age.	Number who complete that year.	Number who died during the next year.
0	10,000	1539
1	8,461	682
2	7,779	505
3	7,274	276
4	6,998	201
5	6,797	121
6	6,676	82
7	6,594	58
8	6,536	43
9	6,493	33
10	6,460	29
11	6,431	31
12	6,400	32
13	6,368	33
14	6,335	35
15	6,300	39
16	6,261	42
17	6,219	43
18	6,176	43
19	6,133	43
20	6,090	43
21	6,047	42

154	1666	75	160	1675	75
151	1512	76	156	1515	76
146	1360	77	146	1359	77
140	1214	78	132	1213	78
134	1073	79	128	1081	79
126	939	80	116	953	80
117	813	81	112	837	81
108	696	82	102	725	82
98	588	83	94	623	83
87	490	84	84	529	84
77	402	85	78	445	85
67	324	86	71	367	86
57	257	87	64	296	87
47	200	88	51	232	88
38	152	89	39	181	89
31	114	90	37	142	90
24	82	91	30	105	91
18	58	92	21	75	92
13	40	93	14	54	93
9	27	94	10	40	94
6	17	95	7	30	95
4	11	96	5	23	96
2	6	97	4	18	97
1	4	98	3	14	98
	2	99	2	11	99
	1	100	2	9	100
	1	101	2	7	101
		102	2	5	102
		103	2	3	103
		104	1	1	104

55	6,497	22	42	6,005	22
56	6,442	23	42	5,963	23
56	6,386	24	42	5,921	24
57	6,329	25	43	5,879	25
58	6,271	26	43	5,836	26
59	6,213	27	45	5,793	27
60	6,154	28	50	5,748	28
60	6,094	29	56	5,698	29
61	6,033	30	57	5,642	30
62	5,971	31	57	5,585	31
63	5,909	32	56	5,528	32
63	5,845	33	55	5,472	33
64	5,782	34	55	5,417	34
65	5,717	35	55	5,362	35
66	5,651	36	56	5,307	36
66	5,585	37	57	5,251	37
67	5,518	38	58	5,194	38
68	5,451	39	61	5,136	39
69	5,382	40	66	5,075	40
69	5,313	41	69	5,009	41
70	5,243	42	71	4,940	42
71	5,173	43	71	4,869	43
71	5,102	44	71	4,798	44
72	5,030	45	70	4,727	45
73	4,957	46	69	4,657	46
73	4,884	47	67	4,588	47
74	4,811	48	63	4,521	48
74	4,736	49	61	4,458	49
75	4,662	50	59	4,397	50
75	4,586	51	62	4,338	51
76	4,511	52	65	4,276	52

TABLE X.—POPULATION OF ST. MARY'S and ST. CUTHBERT'S in 1780, 1788, and 1796.

Townships or Quarters	1780					1788			Between 1780 and 1788		1796					Between 1780 and 1796	
	Houses	Families	Males	Females	Total	Males	Females	Total	Increase	Decrease	Houses	Families	Males	Females	Total	Increase	Decrease
English Street	208	319	639	732	1371	801	1030	1851	480		213	482	738	892	1,630	259	
Scotch Street	122	197	354	437	791	423	530	953	162		140	290	411	504	915	124	
Fisher Street	53	82	130	194	324	143	222	365	41		52	75	134	183	317		7
Castle Street	81	143	220	307	527	320	411	731	204		162	260	379	496	875	348	
Abbey St. and Annetwell St.	77	121	173	270	443	340	521	861	418		78	124	205	276	481	38	
The Abbey	8	8	17	31	48	20	24	44		4	8	8	18	25	43		5
Total within the walls	549	870	1533	1971	3504	2047	2758	4805	1301		675	1239	1885	2376	4,261	757	
Botchergate	95	202	385	457	842	259	329	588		254	172	330	689	762	1,451	609	
Rickergate	82	177	307	356	663	319	367	686	23		124	204	366	445	811	148	
Caldewgate	165	356	592	698	1290	576	705	1281		9	322	541	1010	1183	2,193	903	
Total Suburbs	342	735	1284	1511	2795	1154	1401	2555		240	618	1075	2065	2390	4,455	1660	
Newtown	16	19	40	52	92	...	...	...			23	23	56	58	114	22	
Harraby	9	10	31	41	72	26	26	52		20	8	8	19	32	51		21
Carlton	30	30	66	67	133	91	81	172	39		34	34	99	88	187	54	
Wreay Chapelry	17	18	56	58	114	60	54	114			21	21	60	54	114		
Brisco	32	34	107	85	192	95	89	184		8	34	35	97	94	191		1
Botcherby	21	22	46	52	98	43	46	89		9	19	19	38	40	78		20
Upperby	20	21	35	54	89	44	48	92	3		22	22	44	49	93	4	
Blackhall	63	64	176	178	354	169	151	320		34	70	73	193	185	378	24	
Cummersdale	22	22	60	50	110	105	123	228	118		33	36	112	110	222	112	
Morton Head and Newby	27	27	57	67	124	...	...	...			30	31	75	70	145	21	
Total in Country District	257	267	674	704	1378	633	618	1251		127	294	302	793	780	1,573	195	
Omitted in parts of the City	...	...	...	...	...	30	36	66									
Grand Total	1148	1872	3591	4186	7677	3864	4813	8677	1000		1587	2616	4743	5546	10,289	2612	

N.B.—The Population of Newtown, Morton, and Newby, in 1788, was most probably included in the Returns for Caldewgate and Cummersdale.

TABLE XI.

Number of CHRISTENINGS and DEATHS in both Parishes.

Years.	CHRISTENINGS.				DEATHS.				
	Males.	Females.	Total.	Dissenters.	Males.	Females.	Total.	Increase.	Decrease.
1779	102	109	211	9	133	125	258	...	47
1780	132	120	252	9	108	117	225	27	
1781	136	130	266	9	103	101	204	62	
1782	118	139	257	38	84	122	206	51	
1783	139	123	262	35	85	96	181	81	
1784	121	153	274	36	73	85	158	116	
1785	148	119	267	28	94	110	204	63	
1786	123	103	226	43	100	105	205	21	
1787	145	122	267	51	101	98	199	68	
1788	144	118	262	44	81	106	187	75	
1789	131	109	240	53	107	106	213	27	
1790	107	118	225	49	105	130	235	...	10
1791	129	127	256	67	171	173	344		88
1792	148	137	285	54	109	117	226	59	
1793	141	139	280	48	107	109	216	64	
1794	145	134	279	39	129	130	259	20	
1795	144	122	266	30	131	157	288	...	22
1796	147	149	296	39	141	132	273	23	

TOTAL BETWEEN 1779 AND 1796.

Christenings.

Males . 2410 } 4681
Females 2271 }

Increase in Males 139

Deaths.

Males . 1962 } 4081
Females 2119 }

Males — 157

Births + Deaths = . 600

The Christenings of the Dissenters were not obtained for the years 1779-80-81. They are in the following years included in the columns of the Males and Females.

TABLE XII.

VIEW of the ANNUAL AVERAGE MORTALITY at different
Periods in CARLISLE.

Term.	Commencing with the Year	Ending with the Year	Mean Population.	Died Yearly on an Average.	
				Persons.	One of
9 Years.	1779	1787	8,177	204	40.00
8 Years.	1788	1795	9,458	. 246	38.45
5 Years.	1796	1800	10,667	249.2	42.80
22 Years.	1779	1800	9,209	229.73	40.09
10 Years.	1801	1810	12,660	285.8	44.30

The author of the article "Human Mortality" (*Encyclop. Britan.*,
8th ed., vol. xv. p. 638), after specifying the observations hitherto
published from which the laws of mortality may be correctly determined—namely, those of M. Deparcieux in France, the Swedish,
Dr. Heysham's at Carlisle, Dr. Cleland's at Glasgow, Mr. Finlaison's on the nominees of life annuities granted by Government in
this country, and Mr. Morgan's on the lives insured in the Equitable Assurance Society—goes on to say :—" Those of Deparcieux,
Finlaison, and Morgan, were made only on select classes of people ;
the Swedish are incomparably the most numerous and extensive ;
and whilst Dr. Cleland's exhibit the mortality in a large manu-
facturing town, Dr. Heysham's will, we believe, be found to be
the best authenticated and most correct."

TABLE XIII.

A TABLE exhibiting the POPULATION and MORTALITY at CARLISLE for 35 Years, ending with 1813.

Year	Population	Deaths	One of	
1779	7,677	258	29.76	34
1780	7,739	225	34.40	33
1781	7,864	204	38.55	24
1782	7,989	206	38.78	23
1783	8,114	181	44.83	12
1784	8,239	158	52.15	5
1785	8,364	204	41.00	21
1786	8,489	205	41.41	19
1787	8,614	199	43.29	13
1788	8,805	187	47.09	9
1789	8,996	213	42.24	17
1790	9,187	235	39.09	22
1791	9,378	344	27.26	35
1792	9,569	226	42.34	16
1793	9,760	216	45.19	11
1794	9,951	259	38.42	25
1795	10,145	288	35.23	31
1796	10,316	273	37.79	27
1797	10,487	284	36.93	29
1798	10,658	195	54.66	3
1799	10,829	176	61.53	1
1800	11,000	318	34.59	32
1801	11,300	236	47.88	7
1802	11,600	245	47.35	8
1803	11,900	241	49.38	6
1804	12,200	287	42.51	15
1805	12,500	208	60.10	2
1806	12,800	298	42.95	14
1807	13,100	345	37.97	26
1808	13,400	321	41.75	18
1809	13,800	374	36.90	30
1810	14,060	303	46.40	10
1811	13,680	259	52.82	4
1812	13,957	338	41.29	20
1813	14,257	377	37.64	28

The great increase in the rate of Mortality in 1800 was evidently owing to the great dearth, which produced the same effect all over the Kingdom. The same applies to 1785.

K

Before Dr. Farr constructed the English Life Tables, Professor De Morgan pronounced the " Carlisle Table " to be "the best existing table of healthy life in England." The life assurance offices in the United States of America seem to have endorsed this opinion, and made the same table applicable to their interests. And the magnitude of these interests at home and across the Atlantic, resting entirely on Dr. Heysham's operations, is far beyond ordinary computation.

Dr. Peacock, Dean of Ely, in his life of the famous Dr. Thomas Young, F.R.S., writes—" The experience of the London life offices, of which seventeen had been established a sufficient length of time, in 1843, to afford materials for discussion, has afforded a table of the expectation of life from the age of 20 upwards, so nearly in accordance with the results of the Carlisle Tables, as to leave no doubt of its correctly representing the rate of mortality, for the middle of life, of a past generation, amongst that class of persons who are concerned with insurances on lives ; but the question may reasonably be asked, whether it is equally competent to furnish the value of the expectation for future generations as well as the past " (vol. i. p. 403). The Dean's questioning of the future of the Carlisle Tables was reasonably based on the improvements in the practice of medicine, the increasing temperance and better social habits of the people, and the general adoption of better sanitary arrangements by the country at large.

When the reader reflects on the size of Carlisle, and its suburbs and outlying district, so limited a range for the construction of a mortality Table, and compares it with the basis of the English Life Table, drawn from the mortality of the entire kingdom, he cannot fail to recognise Dr. Heysham's marvellous aptitude and attention. If the records of nine years, extending over a population that did not quite reach 9000, can be shown to vie with the data obtained from the whole community of England and Wales, and over a period of 30 years, not a word more need be said of the care and thorough knowledge Heysham displayed of his subject.

Carlisle, it may be supposed, offered a sanitary condition reflective of England at large. As a city of middle size—the population of its two parishes being five-sixths urban and one-sixth rural—its trading interests demanding a large proportion of operatives ; its crowded lanes, like larger towns, favouring the spread of epidemics, small-pox, fever ; and lastly, but probably first in significance, its large infantile population. These circumstances conspired to make Carlisle a fair epitome of the borough and landed interest, *quoad* the general health of the kingdom.

Though Dr. Heysham ceased to register all the details of the mortality in the way that had engaged him from 1779 to the end of 1787, he still watched the general results in the annual increase of the population, and the annual mortality of Carlisle.

Thus Table X. shows the population of St. Mary's and St. Cuthbert's in 1780, 1788,* and 1796; and Table XI. records the number of christenings and deaths in both parishes.

Wishing to show the annual average mortality at different periods in Carlisle, commencing with the year 1779 and ending with 1810, Table XII. was constructed.

Thirty-five years are summed up in Table XIII.

The many questions arising out of Dr. Heysham's Bills of Mortality, and subsequently his correspondence with Mr. Joshua Milne, are freely discussed in Mr. Milne's able treatise on Life Annuities.

A few more memoranda may not be altogether unacceptable to the reader, seeing that they tend to illustrate Dr. Heysham's painstaking exertions, and characterise the circumstances that affected the rate of mortality towards the close of the last century, also the changes brought about by the discovery of Jenner, and the adoption of hygienic measures, and not less the application of more scientific methods in the treatment of disease.

The accuracy of Dr. Heysham's observations compared with the Government returns is strikingly seen in the following Table, constructed from the seventeen years ending with 1796:—

---

* As before stated, the census was taken in December 1787 ; but as that of 1780 was taken in January of that year, it seemed the best approximation to make the census appear as taken in 1788.

	BAPTISMS.			BURIALS.		
	Males.	Females.	Both.	Males.	Females.	Both.
According to Dr. Heysham . . .	2298	2162	4460	1829	1994	3823
According to the Government Returns .	1864	1772	3636	1798	1946	3744
Omissions in the latter	434	390	824	31	48	79

And in the thirty-one years ending with 1810, the total number of burials in the two parishes of St. Mary's and St. Cuthbert's was—

According to Dr. Heysham . . .	7654
„ „ the Returns to Parliament .	7457
Amount of deficiencies in the latter . .	197

During Dr. Heysham's nine years' observations (1779-1787), when inoculation prevailed, 241 persons died of smallpox; and of these, 228 died under five years of age, eight persons between five and ten years, and only five persons above ten years of age.

Vaccination was introduced in 1800, and twelve years elapsed before a single death occurred in Carlisle from smallpox.

It may interest local readers to know that the population of Carlisle, its suburbs, and villages (St. Mary's and St. Cuthbert's parishes) was 11,094 in 1801, and that it increased up to 13,496 in 1811. At the time of the survey in 1811, the number of families engaged in agriculture was found to be 236, or in the proportion of 78 to 1000 ; the families employed in trade, manufactures, or handicraft, were 2377, or 787 to 1000 ; "all others" not classified in the foregoing divisions, 409, or in the proportion of 135 to 1000 families.

The annual average number of deaths occurring in Carlisle during the first ten years of the present century was 10 out of every 443 of the population ; and, if the deaths from smallpox be excepted, the mortality was exactly the same during the nine years ending with 1787. Owing to a great excess in the number of deaths in 1809, the average was raised.

According to Mr. Milne, when smallpox and typhus fever prevailed, as in the nine years ending with 1787, there would die annually 1 in 40 of the population of Carlisle; after the introduction of vaccination, 1 in 44 ; and, other circumstances being the same, with "little or no mortality from typhus fever, as in the first ten years of the nineteenth century," 1 in 46 of the population.

Dr. Heysham's observations on the comparative mortality of different diseases were all the more valuable that, in the capacity of physician, he could correctly represent the facts, both from his own knowledge and from the reports of his medical friends. The sphere of his survey was so far limited, but this was more than counterbalanced by his perfect knowledge of the district and the people, their callings, and all other circumstances bearing upon the investigation. In his tabulation of the diseases, or specification of the causes of mortality, in noting the different seasons of the year of their occurrence, and in recording the respective numbers of the two sexes, Dr. Heysham shone above all his predecessors, and thereby rendered his work most acceptable and trustworthy. Mr. Milne remarked upon the high value of Dr. Heysham's statements, and their accuracy and minuteness, in part derivable from the moderate size of Carlisle, but mainly owing to the Doctor's zeal and personal acquaintance with all the data, numerical and medical. Except the Swedish returns, Mr. Milne was of opinion that the documents from which the Carlisle Table of Mortality had been formed were " the only data derived from a fluctuating population that have yet been published (1815), which furnish the means of forming an accurate table of mortality."

APPENDIX.

The CORRESPONDENCE between Dr. HEYSHAM and Mr. JOSHUA MILNE, Actuary to the Sun Life Assurance Office, on the CARLISLE BILLS of MORTALITY.

SUN LIFE ASSURANCE OFFICE,
LONDON, 12*th September* 1812.

To Dr. Heysham, Carlisle.

SIR—Being engaged in inquiries relative to Human Mortality, and having met with your valuable Observations thereon, that were published at Carlisle in 1797, I have constructed a Table of Mortality from them, whereby it appears that the inhabitants of your city surpass in longevity those of any other place (so far as I am informed) for which a similar table has yet been constructed.

There are, however, several desiderata, that you may possibly have it in your power to furnish me with, which would enable me to render that Table much more worthy of confidence than I have at present the means of making it.

Under these circumstances, although I have not the honour of your acquaintance, your zeal in the cause of science and humanity, and the liberal and extended views that are unfolded in the little tract above referred to, have emboldened me to take this liberty, in availing myself of my brother's going to Carlisle, to request the favour of your furnishing me with such further information on the subject as it may be agreeable or convenient for you to communicate. As my brother neither understands the subject, nor takes much interest in it, it is necessary that I should write all I have to say ; I must therefore beg your indulgence while I make a few remarks upon the documents I am possessed of, and state some of the difficulties which I hope to overcome through your assistance. As the pamphlet above mentioned is stated to be an *abridgment* of your observations, I hope you may be able to refer my brother to printed information at greater length on the subject, which he will forward me, as I cannot expect you to take the trouble of writing at any great length : but that I may enable you to furnish me with such information as you may not have printed, with as little trouble as possible, I have kept my remarks and queries distinct, and having numbered each of them, have reserved a copy, so that answering them by their numbers you may not have occasion to repeat them.

I can neither expect nor desire that you should go farther into the subject than your taste or your zeal may render agreeable to you ; but any information you may give, should it be ever so little, will be very thankfully received by, Sir,

Your most obedient servant,

JOSHUA MILNE,
Actuary to the Sun Life Office.

Expectation of Life at Carlisle by the Table mentioned within.

Age.	Expectation.
0	39.86
5	51.23
10	48.68
15	44.73
20	41.23
25	37.60
30	34.03
35	30.84
40	27.44
45	24.18
50	21.03
55	17.63
60	14.29
65	11.66
70	9.05
75	6.90
80	5.42
85	4.43
90	3.15
95	1.94
100	.50

By the same Table it appears that out of the whole number born

One of	Attains the Age of
2	43 years.
3	63 ,,
4	69 ,,
10	79 ,,
5000	100 ,,

The Table was constructed from the enumerations of 1780 and 1787, given in Dr. Heysham's 3d Table, and from the Mortality given in the Doctor's 5th and 6th Tables, that took place from the commencement of 1780 to the end of 1787, that of 1779 not being included.

P.S.—I should also be much obliged to Dr. H. for his permission to publish such parts of his Tables, or other information he may be pleased to afford me, as may give the proper degree of authenticity to such documents, and without which no deductions from them could have any just title to the confidence of the public.

REMARKS.

1. The statements of the number of annual deaths at every age under 20 years are as satisfactory as I could desire ; but the number of the still-born is not mentioned.

2. The number of annual christenings brought to account must always be expected to fall short, more or less, of the real number of annual births. The christenings of Dissenters are expressly stated to be included ; but Quakers do not baptize, and there are probably few years or none, in which some children do not die before baptism. I am informed that many poor Irish have settled in Carlisle of late years, much the greater part of whom are, I suppose, Roman Catholics : and it is said that some amongst the indigent classes neglect the rite of baptism altogether, to save the fees.

3. Calculating from the given number of annual christenings, and that of the annual deaths at every age under 5 years, I make the number of the living under that age, about one-tenth part less than it was found to be, by the enumerations of 1780 and 1787.

4. The whole number of the living under 5 years is given, without any specification of the number living in each particular year of age included in that interval.

5. The numbers, as well of the living, as of the annual deaths after 20 years of age, are only given for each interval of ten years, although it is very desirable that they could be obtained for each interval of five.

6. There is also given a statement of the number of the inhabitants in 1796, but the ages are not attended to, neither were they in the Surveys of 1801 and 1811 by order of Government ; but, on some one or more of these occasions, probably Dr. Heysham, or some other gentleman distinguished by the same curiosity and intelligence, may have taken care that the numbers of the living at the different ages should be ascertained, as in the Surveys of 1780 and 1787, or still more minutely ; and the information so obtained would not only be applicable to the most important purposes, but would very much enhance the value of what had been previously published.

QUERIES.

1. May there not have been births of Quakers, Roman Catholics, or others, which are not entered amongst the christenings in Table 8, although the deaths of some of them (under 5) may be entered in Table 5 ; and if so, what may probably be the proportion of these to the whole number of births?

2. May not some of those who migrate into the place in quest of employment, bring children with them under 5, whereby both the number of the deaths, and of the living under that age, may be increased without a corresponding increase of the births ; and what proportion may the number of children so brought in, probably bear to the whole number in the place of that age?

If this and the last Query could be answered with tolerable precision, the difference noticed in the 3d remark might be accounted for, and reduced to little or nothing; then the remarkably small mortality amongst infants in Carlisle might be firmly established.

3. In Table 3, of the number of inhabitants of different ages, the sexes are not distinguished, which is much to be regretted, as we are thereby deprived of the very interesting and curious truths which might otherwise have been deduced from that distinction in the tables of the number dying annually at each age, and of each sex.

Can I be favoured with the numbers of the living thus distributed?

4. In the 10th page of the pamphlet we are informed that Dr. Heysham's tables of the numbers dying of different diseases at each age, are omitted, as wholly appertaining to medical subjects ; but I should set great value upon them.

Could I be favoured with a copy?

Possibly, too, the number of the still-born may there be noticed.

5. If the living at each age were determined according to the 6th Remark, the deaths at all ages from 1787 till the time of such enumeration would be wanted.

Can they be procured?

CARLISLE, *Nov.* 1, 1812.

DEAR SIR—Your brother delivered to me your obliging favour on the 26th of September, and as I presume he will have by this time arrived in London, and put into your hands the volume of observations on the Bills of Mortality, etc., I take the liberty of informing you, you have my full permission to make what use of them you may think proper, and I shall now with pleasure communicate to you all the information in my power with reference to your remarks and queries.

Remark 1st. As the still-born were never entered in the register of deaths, I did not deem it necessary to notice them, and indeed, it would have been difficult to have obtained an accurate account of them.

2d. After the three first years (1779-1782) I think the number of christenings will be nearly correct, and will fall very little short of the number of living births, as I made it my business to gain the best information on the subject from every species of Dissenters. Although the Quakers do not baptize, they keep a regular register of births, which is annually transmitted from the different preaching houses in the country to the general meeting in London. With respect to the Established Church, I prevailed on our clergy to register all the private baptisms, which had not been the case before, and at that period we had scarcely one Roman Catholic family in the place. It is since that period that the great influx of the lower ranks of Irish Catholics has taken place.

4th and 5th. The information required in these remarks cannot, I am sorry, be obtained.

6th. The same difficulty occurs here. The Survey of 1796 was made by the editors of the *History of Cumberland*, and was, I believe, partly correct as to numbers, but no notice was taken of ages. The Survey of 1801, I have reason to think, was made in a slovenly manner ; that of 1811 is tolerably accurate ; you will find it pasted on the inside of the back of the observations.

Query 1. This is answered in a great measure by what I have observed on remark 2d.

2. There can be no doubt that, between 1779 and 1787, some few parents would bring with them into Carlisle children under 5 years of age ; and, on the contrary, others would take children of the same age away with them, but what were the exact respective numbers of each at this distance of time cannot be ascertained ; it may, however, be observed that the migration into, and emigration, was not very considerable during this period.

3. I am sorry I neglected to distinguish the ages of the different sexes.

4. You will find the Table of deaths and diseases of persons of different ages in the book I sent by your Brother, for every year except 1780, which, on examination, I found is wanting, and for that table I have made the most diligent search, but in vain.

5. The information required cannot be procured.

You will observe, by examining the Table of deaths and diseases of persons of different ages, that, in 8 years, 238 children, chiefly under 5 years of age,

tables of the number of annual deaths at every age afford the most indubitable
proofs of a singularly small mortality amongst the general mass of the inhabitants of Carlisle. You may perhaps indeed only mean that, as you have not
been in the habit of keeping any register of the number of your departed
friends, you had no idea before how much you had been favoured yourself in
surviving so many of them.

But, to facilitate to you the determination of the question whether or no
the mortality has been greater amongst your friends than the general mass of
the population of the same ages in and about your city are subject to, I insert
this little Table :

Out of 100 living in Carlisle at the age of	30	35	40	45	50	55	60	65
The number that survive 30 years is .	64	56	47	35	21	11	4	1
Being then aged respectively . .	60	65	70	75	80	85	90	95

If the respectable gentlemen you mention have gone more quickly off the
stage, you will probably think with me, that inactivity and repletion may have
accelerated their course in comparison with that of their poor neighbours.

I acknowledge that it is altogether unreasonable in me to give you further
trouble after what you have already had. But if you should take sufficient
interest in the question yourself, you would oblige me by informing me at your
leisure, how you consider the industrious classes of the people in and about
Carlisle, and especially the labouring poor, to have been circumstanced, as to
the facility of obtaining a subsistence, during the nine years in which your
observations were made, in comparison with their general circumstances for
the whole time within your memory or knowledge.

The general rate of mortality that results from your observations, corresponds very exactly with that which, in my opinion, may be legitimately deduced
from the enumeration of the people, and the extracts from the parish registers
throughout England and Wales, that were printed by order of Parliament in
1802 and 1812 ; but it is considerably less than that of any town in Britain
wherein such observations have hitherto been made, or than the general mortality
of any foreign country except North America, where the incessantly increasing
demand for labour has greatly meliorated the condition of the people. As the
number of persons In the class above referred to is incomparably greater than
in those above them, the general results of such tables must always depend
principally upon them, and therefore a continually increasing demand for labour
for a certain period, might keep the rate of mortality during its continuance

materially below the level at which it might have stood, both before that encouragement had been held out, and after it was withdrawn.

Thus it is obvious that, if the period intervening between the years 1778 and 1788 should have *accidentally* been one of great prosperity and increasing opulence in Carlisle, it might be very unsafe to draw any conclusions as to future events from Tables depending upon such accidental data. I have not the least reason to think that has been the case, but both on account of your judgment and your accurate local knowledge, your sentiments on the subject would be highly esteemed by, dear Sir, yours, etc.　　　　　　JOSHUA MILNE.

CARLISLE, *February* 6, 1813.

MY DEAR SIR—You will recollect that my Observations were published during a period of war, and in that respect similar to the present times ; but perhaps you may not recollect that during the American war the price of all the necessaries of life was extremely different from what it has generally been during the present war. But if at that time food was cheap, wages were also low, and I think that the labouring classes have lived better during the last fifteen years (the years of scarcity excepted) than from 1778 to 1788, and I am also of opinion that the mortality of late has been diminished. In my former communication I have stated the difference with respect to the smallpox among children, and I have now to inform you that, for the last fifteen years, we have had, notwithstanding the great increase of population, very few cases of typhus, a disease, as you will see by examining the Tables, in a great measure fatal to adults. No less than 119 died of that disease during the nine years. This number I have been able to ascertain, though the Table for 1780 is lost, having noticed in the body of the Observations that three died of that disease in that year. Therefore, taking it for granted that the mortality from all the other disorders remains nearly the same, it is evident the general mortality must be diminished from the absence of these two fatal complaints, the first chiefly to children and the second to adults. In order, however, to enable you to judge of our present situation, it occurred to me, upon the receipt of your last favour, that you might derive benefit from a statement of the Bills of Mortality for the year 1812. I have selected 1812 in preference to 1811, when the last survey took place, because that year was peculiarly healthy, no epidemic of any kind having appeared ; whereas, I apprehend 1812 may be esteemed a pretty fair average year (notwithstanding the very high price of provisions), two epidemic diseases having prevailed—namely, the measles and the hooping-cough. The measles commenced in the latter end of June or beginning of July, and as that disorder

L

had not visited Carlisle for several years, there were a large number of children liable to infection. The disease was consequently very general ; I conceive upwards of 1000 were affected. The epidemic, however, was extremely mild, and considering the number affected few died. Before I offer any observations on the christenings and burials, I will give you a comparative statement of the deaths in the parish of St. Cuthbert in the last two years. In 1811 the deaths were only 97 ; in 1812 they amounted to 151.

Before the returns of the survey of 1811 were transmitted to the proper office in London, I examined them with great care, and found the population of the two parishes of St. Cuthbert and St. Mary, Carlisle, to be 13,495. I deemed it, however, prudent to delay writing to you till I had an opportunity of comparing my account with the account published by Government ; and as our clerk of the peace, to whom the work was transmitted, does not reside in Carlisle, I did not receive it till within these few days. On examination, I found a difference of *one*, which difference occurs at Harraby, where I make the inhabitants 57, the printed work makes them 58 ; this error has either arose from the enumeration or the press. As you are no doubt in possession of the work, by referring to page 49, letters (l) and (m), and to page 54 summary, city of Carlisle, you will find the population to be 13,496, I shall therefore take them at that number. In 1812, the 55th Regiment of Foot and a troop of the 2d Dragoon Guards were stationed at Carlisle, amounting to 300 men, and some of these men had wives and families ; but as both regiments have lately been removed, it is impossible to ascertain the exact number of wives and children, and as it will be perhaps best to err on the safe side, I shall consider the population at 13,796. The burials are accurate, but I apprehend the christenings will fall considerably short of the births. The minister of one of the Dissenting congregations was taken ill early on and died before the conclusion of the year, and no successor has yet been appointed. We have also a small number of Anabaptists, who, I understand, do not baptize children. With respect to the Established Church, although there are no fees paid for christening, yet here, as in most other places, the parents give an entertainment to their friends on the occasion ; many, I understand, delayed the ceremony last year on account of the distressed state of the times.

·· Of the number of christenings 3 were Quakers,* 15 were Presbyterians, and 48 were Catholics—total 66.

* Dr. Heysham must have meant three births among the Quaker body, as Quakers do not baptize.

The following statements regarding the Births and Burials in Carlisle were sent to Mr. Milne on the 6th February 1813 :—

	Males.	Females.	Total.
Baptisms—Saint Mary's . .	123	105	228
Saint Cuthbert's .	89	99	1°8
Wreay Chapel . .	5	5	10
Births among Quakers . .	2	1	3
Baptisms—Roman Catholics .	25	23	48
Presbyterians and others	8	7	15
	252	240	492

	Males.	Females.	Total.
Burials—Saint Mary's .	81	101	182
Saint Cuthbert's .	76	75	151
Wreay Chapel	1	0	1
Quakers .	2	2	4
	160	178	338

Excess of Births over Burials   154

	Males.	Females.	Total.
Deaths in 1812 .	160	178	338
Christenings in 1812 .	252	240	492
Deaths in St. Cuthbert's		151	
Deaths in St. Mary's		187	
		338	

Should you require any further explanation you may command my services. —I remain, dear Sir, yours, etc.   J. HEYSHAM.

SUN LIFE OFFICE, 13*th Feb.* 1813.

DEAR SIR—I received in due course your obliging favour of the 6th inst., and beg leave to thank you in the kindest manner for the great and successful pains you have taken to satisfy the inquiries I troubled you with.

I shall always consider myself to have been peculiarly fortunate in having procured the assistance of a gentleman whose zeal disposes him, no less than his abilities qualify him, to render it of the most effectual kind. I am in possession of all that has been printed by order of Parliament on the population of the kingdom, and the numbers of annual baptisms, burials, etc., for the last century.

I did not fail to compare those for Carlisle with your valuable Tables, and had
the satisfaction to find that your numbers were always the greatest, consequently
your omissions (if any) the least ; in the number of burials the difference is
generally small, but in the baptisms almost always considerable.

I have also compared the statement of the population in your last favour
with the parts of the last published " Abstract, etc.," which you referred me to,
and find it perfectly correct.

I am particularly obliged to you for the baptisms and burials of the last year,
and am much gratified to find the mortality so small, even in a year of hardship
and scarcity that succeeded several of prosperity and plenty.

Drs. Haygarth and Percival, many years ago, began to remark a gradual
diminution in the general mortality, as may be seen in their excellent papers in
the *Philosophical Transactions;* Dr. W. Heberden, in his tract on the Increase
and Decrease of Diseases, showed that it still continued to decrease, not only
here, but in the principal cities of Europe, though more slowly ; and there is, I
think, every reason to expect that, as the arts and manufactures approach per-
fection, and a taste for their productions diffuses itself lower and lower amongst
the industrious classes, the ravages of putrid and pestilential diseases will
diminish. But while such nests of poverty, wretchedness, and pestilence, still
exist in crowded cities, as that wherein you state the jail-fever of Carlisle to have
been engendered, in your valuable and interesting tract on that subject, and
which the late and much to be lamented Dr. Willan, in his work on the Diseases
of London, shows to be still but too common in this metropolis, the general mortality in great towns must, I fear, continue to be much higher than in your
favoured city. I beg pardon both for the haste and carelessness wherewith I
write to you, and for the digression I have insensibly wandered into.

It remains only that I thank you for your obliging offer to continue your
valuable communications in case I find myself under the necessity of troubling
you again ; and I remain, dear Sir,

Your much obliged, etc.,

JOS. MILNE.

SUN LIFE OFFICE, 31*st December* 1813.

DEAR SIR—In consequence of your obliging offer to give me any further information I might want, I trouble you once more.

You no doubt think me slow ; but I have not been idle. I have experienced
considerable difficulty in getting the algebraical part of the work I have in hand

printed to my mind ; it is now, however, about half finished, and I hope to publish early in the spring.

I am just now entering upon the popular part, where I have occasion to show upon what authorities the Tables depend, and to compare the mortality at Carlisle with that which the late returns to Government from all parts of England and Wales exhibit.

It will be useful, too, to compare the present mortality at Carlisle with that which prevailed during the time of your observations. This, I think, will be best done by taking the annual average number of deaths during the five years, whereof 1811 was the middle one, and comparing that with the number 13,796, which (including the military, with their wives and children) you consider to have been the actual population in 1811.

No safe inference can be drawn from the mortality of a single year ; but if you consider the addition of 300 for the military to raise the population too high *for the average* of these *five years,* I have to beg you would be kind enough to say what number you consider to approach nearer the truth.

The part of the requisite information which I already have I insert here, that you may correct it if you find it necessary ; and hope you will be able, without much trouble, to supply the number of deaths in 1811 and 1813.

	Deaths of		Births.	Authorities.
	Males.	Females.		
1809	155	210	365	} Returns to Go-
1810	147	148	295	} vernment.
1811	127	132	259	*
1812	160	178	338	Your favour of
				6th Feb. last.
1813	188	189	3 77	*

If the distinction of the sexes be attended with any trouble whatever, pray omit it, and I am not much concerned about the christenings.

To a work just published by Dr. Watt of Glasgow, on " The History of Nature and Treatment of Chincough," there is subjoined, " An Inquiry into the

* The information asked for by Mr. Milne for the years 1811 and 1813, I have taken the liberty of inserting along with the other returns ; it is contained in Dr. Heysham's letter of January 23, 1814.

Relative Mortality of the principal Diseases of Children, and the number who have died under ten years of age in Glasgow during the last thirty years," by which it appears that smallpox still occasions some mortality there, and that the mortality from measles has increased almost as much as that from smallpox has diminished. The work, I think, cannot fail to interest you, and lest you should not at present possess it, I beg leave to hand you an extract which contains what is most material with regard to the changes that have taken place in the relative mortality of the diseases of children. Pray favour me with your sentiments on the prevalence and the fatality of measles, or any other diseases which may have appeared to increase, either in the degree of their mortality, or the frequency of their occurrence, since the introduction of vaccination. I hope, too, to hear none have died of the smallpox in 1813.

From your information respecting hooping-cough and measles in your favour of February last, I have little doubt but that your case in Carlisle has not been similar to theirs in Glasgow.

In the work I am employed upon I shall have occasion to notice some of the results of inquiries which have been made, in Sweden, into the relative mortality of different diseases, where registers have been kept of the numbers that have died of each disease throughout the whole kingdom (consisting of a population of three millions) for more than 20 years.

I find that *the remittent Fever of Infants*, which they express by the single word *Alta*, makes a conspicuous figure. You have probably seen a pamphlet published by the late *Dr. Rutter*, on this disease, in 1782 (2d edition in 1806) ; and *Mr. Coley*, a surgeon at Bridgenorth, has just published a work on the same subject. Pray inform me if what you have called, and has been generally called, worm-fever, be not the same, and whether you would wish me to call it *the infantile remittent fever* in what you have authorised me to print. Uniformity of nomenclature and classification, certainly, is very desirable in such Tables, which otherwise lose half their value, from the difficulty of comparing them with each other.

By forwarding such information as it may be convenient for you to collect, or to communicate at the earliest opportunity, will yet further oblige,

Dear Sir, yours already obliged, etc.,

JOS. MILNE.

23d January 1814.

DEAR SIR — I received your favour of the 31st of December, and, with pleasure, communicate every information in my power, and am glad to find your work will be published in the course of this season.

With respect to any increase in the mortality of measles, I have not observed it here any further than, in consequence of no deaths from smallpox, a greater number of children will be liable to be infected with that disease when it prevails, than would have been the case had a considerable number of them been carried off by smallpox. So far with respect to the facts, and in what manner vaccination can predispose the bodies of children to be more severely affected by measles I do not pretend to know. From the extract you have enclosed, I find the measles have been epidemic every year from 1807 to 1812 in Glasgow—namely, 6 years. Such is not the case either in Carlisle or in the county of Cumberland, the disorder generally only appearing about every 4, 5, or 6 years.

The scarlet fever, certainly, occurs more frequently of late than was formerly the case, but then it does not spread so extensively, and, I apprehend, taking into consideration the difference of population, it is not more fatal than it was during the period I published the Observations.

I have not had an opportunity of seeing the works you allude to on the subject of infantile diseases, but am disposed to believe that worms (the tape excepted) are not attended with very fatal consequences ; when, however, they exist in the intestines, some are generally expelled in almost all febrile diseases, and hence they have, by the vulgar, been considered as the cause. I therefore see no objection to your altering the designation.

In the beginning of September last a poor woman from Scotland, with her child just recovered from the smallpox, came to a lodging-house in one of our suburbs, and communicated the infection to some children residing under the same roof ; from these, others in the neighbourhood caught the disorder, to the number of 12 or 14—of them two died. By having recourse to vaccination, the progress of the disease was soon checked—no one case having occurred since the beginning of December. These two are the only deaths from smallpox in Carlisle since vaccination was introduced. Subjoined you will find an *accurate* account of the deaths in 1809, 1810, 1811, and 1813; the numbers do not agree with the Government returns, which, I apprehend, you will seldom find correct, even with respect to burials, and still seldomer with respect to christenings. The difference here, I apprehend, arises from the burials of Quakers having been omitted. It is somewhat unfortunate that during this period, considerable fluctuations have taken place in the population of Carlisle. I am perfectly satisfied our population was the greatest in the year 1809, and until the month of September 1810. During that month a sudden and almost total

suppression of the manufactures of this city took place ; in consequence a very
great number of families were thrown out of employment, which occasioned a
considerable emigration. I am of opinion no less than 1000 inhabitants left
Carlisle between the 1st of October 1809 and the latter end of March 1811 ;
however, to be on the safe side, I would advise you to take them at 600. The
survey ordered by Government was made in April 1811, when the emigration had
ceased, and I conceived the population remained nearly stationary from that period
to the latter end of 1812, when, from the patriotism and valour of the Russians,
trade and manufactures began to move, and are now in full vigour ; and I think
you may safely take the increase in 1813 at 500. In 1809, 1810, and 1811 we
had full 100 soldiers, which will make 700 in the two first years to be added to
the population of 1811, and 100 to that year. The 74th Regiment succeeded
the 55th Regiment, which, with detachments and recruiting parties, made the
Garrison full 300, independent of soldiers' wives and families, during the last
year. I therefore consider the population of Carlisle for the last five years to be
as follows,—namely, in

1809.	Resident Inhabitants - - - - -	14,096
	Soldiers - - - - - -	100
		14,196

1810.	Resident Inhabitants - - - - -	14,096
	Soldiers - - - - - -	100
		14,196

1811.	Resident Inhabitants - - - -	13,496
	Soldiers - - - - - -	100
		13,596

1812.	Resident Inhabitants - - - - -	13,496
	Soldiers - - - -	300
		13,796

1813. Resident Inhabitants -   -   -   -   -   13,996
      Soldiers   -   -   -   -   -   -   300

                               14,296

Now, as the emigration took place in the last three months of 1810 and the first three months of 1811, some calculation will be required, and, as you are a much better calculator than I am, I leave that point for you to settle. I also think it proper to remark that in burials three were the consequence of executions,—namely, two in 1809, and one in 1813.

BURIALS.

	Males.		Females.		Total.
1809	-	158	-	216	-	374
1810	-	148	-	155	-	303
1811	-	127	-	132	-	259
1812	-	160	-	178	-	338
1813	-	188	-	189	-	377

                                   —— 1651.

With kind wishes for the success of your work, I remain, dear Sir, yours, etc.,

                                 JOHN HEYSHAM.

           SUN LIFE OFFICE, 14*th February* 1814.

DEAR SIR—I beg leave to trespass once more upon your patience, in consequence of having (in Dr. Willan's work on Vaccination) met with an extract of a letter from you, dated 14th May 1806, wherein there is this passage :— "Since the introduction of vaccination into this city, the smallpox has occasionally occurred, but has never raged as an epidemic, and the mortality from that disease has been very inconsiderable, compared with what it used to be before the introduction of vaccination," which does not appear to agree exactly with the information you were so kind as to favour me with on the 1st November 1812 ; that, " since the introduction of vaccination in 1800, you had reason to believe that not one person had died of the smallpox in Carlisle." Probably you were led to this belief by inquiries subsequent to the date of the above extract from Dr. Willan ; I think it fortunate, however, that I have met with that extract, as, had I published the other statement without being aware of *it*, the apparent contradiction might have shaken the confidence of some persons in the other valuable documents which I owe to your zeal and intelligence.

Although the sexes are not distinguished in your Tables of the Mortality from different diseases, yet that produced by such as are peculiar to females, may, I suppose, be extracted, and would be useful to me ; but I am under some uncertainty with regard to two of these. One person is reported to have died between 40 and 50, " of a discharge of blood ;" was that uterine hæmorrhagy ?

And five of cancer, between 70 and 80 ; can you inform me if any of these 5 cases were cancer of the breasts, or of the uterus?

. I have the satisfaction to inform you that, upon consulting the London bills for the last 14 years, I find that there is no such increase of the mortality from measles as that which Dr. Watt has found in the Glasgow bills.

By favouring me, when convenient, with the desired information on these subjects, you will again do a grateful service to, dear Sir, yours, etc.

JOS. MILNE.

[Dr. Heysham's reply dated 18th February, has been lost.]

SUN LIFE OFFICE, *24th February* 1814.

DEAR SIR—I have now to acknowledge the receipt of your esteemed favour of the 18th instant, with information that is perfectly satisfactory as to the chief object of inquiry in my last ; the others (which indeed I knew it was not likely that you should be able to satisfy) are of very little importance to me.

I am only sorry that you should have taken so much trouble, as Dr. Willan appears to have printed the whole of your letter, although in his work it is only stated to be an extract from it.—I remain, dear Sir, yours, etc.   JOS. MILNE.

SUN LIFE OFFICE, *March 22d,* 1814.

DEAR SIR—In endeavouring to determine the rate of mortality at Carlisle, with the degree of accuracy which I doubt not but that you are desirous of as well as me, I find that there are still a few points on which my information is defective ; and, after the zeal you have already manifested in promoting the inquiry, I am satisfied that no apology is necessary for troubling you again.

You know that according to the Act (51 G. III. cap. 6) directing the survey of 1811, an answer to the following question was to be returned to government :

" How many persons (etc.) are there actually found in your parish or place, etc. *exclusive of men actually serving in His Majesty's Regular Forces, in the Old Militia, or in any embodied Militia, and exclusive of Seamen either in His Majesty's service, or belonging to Registered Vessels?"* And the same descriptions of persons were directed to be excluded from the returns of 1801. In the Population abstract, $\frac{1}{25}$th is estimated to be the proper addition to the *returned numbers*, in order to obtain the whole population for England and Wales ; and for the Metropolis, they increased the returned number in each case by its twenty-fifth part. The returned population of your two parishes (omitting Middlesceugh and Braythwaite) was—

in 1801 . 11,060 ; and

in 1811 . 13,496.*

The mean population (returnable according to the Act) was therefore, during these 10 years, 12,278 ; and if we increase this by $\frac{1}{25}$th, namely 409, the true mean population will appear to have been 12,687.

But I should think $\frac{1}{25}$th too great an addition for Carlisle, and your accurate information will no doubt enable you to estimate the proper addition much more nearly.

The great fluctuation in your population since October 1810, prevents me from determining the rate of mortality by means of the annual deaths you favoured me with on the 23d January last, as I could have done had the number of the people either remained stationary or varied uniformly. I must therefore have recourse to the two enumerations in 1801 and 1811, thence determine the mean number of the living during the intervening 10 years, and divide it by the annual average number of deaths in the same period. Those for 1809 and 1810, you have already favoured me with, and it is very desirable that I should obtain the exact numbers for the first eight years of the ten ; for I find that the returns to government are not sufficiently accurate to answer my purpose ; the number of deaths in your two parishes in the 17 years ending with 1796, were, according to the Population Abstract—

	Males.	Females.	Total.
	1798	1946	3744
but according to your tables they were .	1829	1994	3823

But as I do not know what trouble it might cost you to furnish me the numbers of deaths in 1801, 1802, 1803, 1804, 1805, 1806, 1807, and 1808, with the same accuracy as the information you have already favoured me with, I do not think it reasonable to ask it, but will leave it to your own determination, and shall be perfectly well satisfied with what you have already done, should you decline it.

* " I will take care to increase this number by 600, according to your advice in your favour of the 23d January last."

Although I know that no one else would perform the task so well as yourself, yet if you know any one that you can depend upon, and who will accept of a compensation for their trouble in furnishing this, or any other information of the kind, that you conceive may be useful to me, I shall be very happy to pay them on their own terms ; and shall be much obliged by your employing them accordingly.

I believe that the mortality in moderate-sized towns like Carlisle, with flourishing manufactures, is much less in comparison with that of country parishes and villages than has generally been supposed ; and I have reason to believe that the law of mortality in your two parishes has, for the last thirty years, been very nearly the same as the average of the kingdom.

But it is very desirable to determine this as nearly as possible. There are no adequate data for instituting a comparison *at the time your Observations were made;* but the late surveys afford the means of doing so, for the term of ten years that intervened between them : *Provided only* that, by means of the data I now trouble you about, we could determine what the rate of mortality really was in your two parishes during the same period. Then, by means of your Tables of the ravages of diseases, and your more recent information respecting vaccination and typhus fever ; it might be shown that, from 1779 to 1787, the mortality was the same, excepting so far as smallpox and typhus increased it.

This would not only afford useful information to the public, but would establish the reputation of your valuable Observations, and contribute to that of the many Tables I have derived from them and am about to print.

You inform me that, within the last fifteen years, very few cases of typhus have occurred ; can you form any estimate of the deaths it has produced in the same time or their annual average number? Can you assign the reason of the disease having become less frequent?

By Sir F. M. Eden's " *State of the Poor*," I find you used to exclude all infectious diseases from the poor-house. Have you any separate fever wards or house of recovery, as they have at Chester, Manchester, Liverpool, London, etc.? Your own tract on the Jail Fever, the writings of Dr. Haygarth, the collection of papers published by Dr. Clark at Newcastle in 1802 (who, I see, consulted you), and the labours of many other eminent physicians, must, no doubt, have contributed greatly to improve the methods both of prevention and cure in such cases, and must thereby have sensibly reduced the general mortality of the kingdom.

Dr. Jenner's first work on Vaccination was, you know, published in 1798, and the House of Recovery, in the metropolis, for the prevention and cure of infectious fevers, was opened in 1802.

	Smallpox.	Fevers of all kinds.	
According to the Bills of Mortality, there died in the ten years ending with 1800, of .	18,477	19,884	
In the ten years ending with 1813 . .	11,228	11,172	Sum.
Difference of the two equal periods ˙ ˙ .	7,249	8,712	15,961

Before I close this long letter, allow me to state distinctly the queries I now trouble you with, and number them ; then, by answering me according to the numbers, you will be spared the trouble of transcribing the queries, as on a former occasion.

1. At what number do you estimate the amount of omissions (according to the Act), in the return of the population of your two parishes in 1801 ?

2. And at what number in 1811 ?

3. At what time of the year was the enumeration of 1801 made ?

4. What was the true number of deaths in each of the eight years 1801—1808 ?

5. Probable number of deaths by typhus fever during the last sixteen years ?

6. Reason of that disease having become less frequent ?

7. The population of your villages appears to have been 400 less in 1811 than in 1780 : has not this been occasioned by some of them having in the intermediate time been included in the suburbs, and so been returned as part of the city ?

8. Towards the end of your Observations you say the deaths by accidents were omitted in a few of the first years. Were not these omissions *in the Tables of diseases only?* Were not all the burials that took place in these years included in the other Tables of the deaths at different ages ?—I remain, dear Sir, yours, etc. JOS. MILNE.

P.S.—You will be pleased to observe, Sir, that according to the present method of instituting the inquiry, we shall have nothing to do with the soldiers (or others) who might be resident in Carlisle *after* the enumeration in April 1811 ; and if the 100 military who were there in 1809 and 1810, were the only persons of that description who were there during the ten years, then we must add but twenty to the mean permanent population for them, as they were but

one-fifth of the time in the place. The increase of deaths from them could therefore be only one-fifth of what they would have been had they remained there
till the ten years had expired. [Here a portion of the manuscript is destroyed ;
then come the words " regular forces;" two more words are wanting ; then fol-
low " ten years, I must request you would have the goodness to give the duration
of their continuance as near as you can."]

The other persons omitted, according to the Act, would, I suppose, shift
about much less. From the reluctance I felt at troubling you any further, I
had prepared this part of my work for the press ; but having at last resolved
upon this step, I shall suspend it until I am favoured with your answer, and
then do that part of it over again.

[Dr. Heysham's letter of 29th March is wanting.]

CARLISLE, *April* 1, 1814.

DEAR SIR—Having half-an-hour's time to spare, I inform you that I have
consulted my medical friends respecting Query 5, and we agree in opinion that
the average number of deaths from typhus during that period will scarcely
amount to *one* each year.

Q. 6. On this subject I cannot satisfy my own mind ; we must therefore rest
satisfied with the fact.

The people in general certainly pay more attention to cleanliness, and upon
the whole live better than they did ; yet during the period of sixteen or seventeen
years we have had several years of scarcity, and some of great distress from want
of employment.

Q. 7. You have here, I apprehend, made a complete mistake. In 1780 there
were in the villages only 1378 persons, whereas, in 1811 there were 1850 ; though
Newtown, the population of which was in 1780, 92, was, in the Survey of 1811,
united with Caldew-gate, one of the suburbs. When on this subject, it may be
necessary to state that, in my Survey, the population of *Newtown* and *Morton
Head, comprehending Newby,* was distinct, but the two *Blackhills, or Black
Halls—namely, high and low—*were united. Whereas, in the Survey 1811,
New Town was united with Caldew-gate ; *Morton Head, comprehending Newby,*
was united with Cummersdale, and the two Blackhills, or Black Halls, were
separated.

8. The deaths from accidents were always included in the number of burials,
and were inserted in the Tables, but were excluded in my calculations to ascertain the comparative mortality of different ages, etc., till 1785. In 1780, for

instance, I have stated that 1 in 34½ nearly, of all the inhabitants have died this year in consequence of *diseases,* and under 5 years old, 1 in 9 and 9-11ths nearly ; between 5 and 10, 1 in 56¾, etc.

1785.—During this year 1 in 37 and 1-7th, nearly, of *all the inhabitants, have died,** and under 5 years old 1 in 10 and 2-3ds nearly ; between 5 and 10, 1 in 151 and 1-3d.

Almost immediately after I wrote to you in January, a woman with a child in the smallpox, after begging in various parts of Carlisle, came to my house to get a pass. I ordered her to leave the town without delay. She had, however, communicated the infection, and the smallpox soon after reappeared ; many, however, have not been affected, and none have yet died ; but unfortunately a boy, aged 9 years, who was vaccinated in October 1805 by one of our most intelligent and attentive surgeons, is now labouring under the confluent smallpox.

You are no doubt acquainted with several members of Parliament ; I therefore request you will authorise me to enclose my future letters to some one or more of them ; till then I remain, dear Sir, yours, etc.,　　　　J. HEYSHAM.

SUN LIFE OFFICE, 2d April 1814.

Dear Sir—I feel much obliged by your kind note of the 29th ult., the more especially as it shows that you sympathise with me in the solicitude with which I look for your aid ; I have myself to blame for not looking more minutely into those parts of the subject before I came actually to reduce the materials into order, and apply them to use : however, I cannot but acquiesce, both cheerfully and thankfully, in the very reasonable delay which your much more important avocations render necessary ; and the great object is to have the thing done well rather than hastily.

When I troubled you on the 22d March, I had not your Observations at hand, but I recollected that the doubt expressed in my 8th query had some time before occurred to me, and I had deferred inquiring particularly into it ; however, in a few hours after I had despatched that letter I satisfied myself that the omission of the deaths by accidents, mentioned at the head of the 10th page of the abridgment of your observations, took place only in calculating the number for your 7th Table.

Upon referring to my own papers, indeed, I find that in reducing all your valuable Tables of diseases into one, I had compared the totals of the deaths in

---

* Deaths by accidents are included in the calculation this year, which have hitherto been omitted.

every interval of age with those in your 5th and 6th Tables, after deducting the deaths in 1780, and find them to agree exactly.

The 4th question put to the Clergymen of England, under the Act 41 G. III. cap. 15, demanded the number of baptisms and burials, both of males and females, for *each* year, only from 1780, inclusive, downwards. You have already printed the numbers, according to your accurate researches, to 1796; those I particularly want, and which I troubled you about in my last letter, would carry these down to the end of the year 1810, that is as far as the Government returns yet go, provided that those for the years 1797, 1798, 1799, and 1800 were also supplied. Those four years, however, are not essential to my purpose, and I leave it entirely to you to do what you think best ; after observing that it is my intention to print your numbers along with those returned to Government, by which the greater accuracy of yours will be made manifest, and the means will be afforded of estimating the probable amount of the omissions in the Government returns generally, so far as two parishes only can furnish these means.

We should then be enabled to determine the rate of mortality in each of the four intervals, 1780-1787, 1787-96, 1796-1801, and 1801-1810 ; between the five enumerations, from the beginning of 1780 down to the end of 1810.

I also purpose reprinting most of your observations very nearly as they stand in the abridgment, in order to give the fullest and clearest information I can, respecting the population of Carlisle, during the time in which your observations were made, and shall therefore be happy to receive any instructions you may favour me with, either as to alterations or additions, and remain, Sir, yours, etc.   JOS. MILNE.

SUN LIFE OFFICE, *4th April* 1814.

DEAR SIR—As I could not find a member in town on Saturday, I had delayed the enclosed for a "frank," which indeed I am not yet certain that I shall obtain to-day, but they shall both go with the first I can get.

This morning I am favoured with yours of the 1st instant, still I had rather let mine of the 2d go, as it will explain how I came to give you unnecessary trouble.

I beg you to accept of my best thanks for your last information respecting smallpox and vaccination, as well as your answers to my 5th, 6th, 7th, and 8th queries.

On the subject of smallpox, I have the pleasure to remark to you, that by having mentioned in your Observations (Abridgment, p. 9) that 90 died of that disease in 1779, and only 151 in the eight succeeding years, it follows that 241 died of it in the whole period of nine years, but in the eight for which your Tables of diseases are preserved, its victims were 238 ; therefore in the year 1780, for which the table is lost, only 3 must have died of it. [This surmise of Mr. Milne's was correct.—H. L.]

In consulting the Population Abstracts of 1801 and 1811, I was a little puzzled, not only by the differences you have been kind enough to explain, but by some of what were termed villages, in your survey of 1780, and kept separate both from the city and suburbs, being included in *the city of Carlisle* in the returns to government (as printed). Thus, Botcherby, Cummersdale, and Brisco, with others, are all enumerated under the head *City of Carlisle;* they are indeed called townships, but so are Castle Street, English Street, Fisher Street, etc. called, and it does not appear by these printed statements whether these streets, or the places above mentioned, are the most centrical with regard to the city.

To explain myself fully, I beg leave to state the population of your two parishes (excepting Middlescough and Braithwaite) ; the sexes need not be dis-tinguished.

1811.	Inhabitants in Blackwell, High	253
„	Blackwell, Low	149
„	Carleton	173
„	Harraby	58
„	Upperby	228
„	Wreay	104

Thus there would appear to be only   965
In the villages, and in the city of Carlisle, there are stated to be . 12,531

                                  13,496

I beg that you would take no further trouble about this part of the subject ; my principal reason for putting the query was with a view to the difference between the proportion of males to females, in the city and suburbs, and in the neighbouring villages.

I should value your communications low indeed if I could consider them expensive, whatever weight you might send me by post under one cover, without any privilege ; but if you will have the goodness to address them to John Irving, Esq., M.P., London, with J. M. under the seal, they will reach me in safety.—I remain, dear Sir, yours, etc. JOS. MILNE.

                                    M

CARLISLE, *April* 10*th*, 1814.

DEAR SIR—I was favoured with yours of the 2d and 4th instant, the day before yesterday, and now enclose the register of the burials for the year 1801 to 1808, which you may depend on being perfectly correct, and which will answer your 4th query. The enclosed surveys of 1780 and 1811 will throw light upon the observations I made in my last letter on your 8th query, as they will give you a clear view of that subject. In a former letter I stated that the survey of 1811 was made in April of that year, which was only partly the case, as a considerable part of St. Cuthbert's was not finished till 27th of May, when the emigration had nearly ceased, and when the population was about the least. I am happy to inform you that Master Hodgson, who was affected with confluent smallpox, after being vaccinated, is perfectly recovered ; and it is somewhat remarkable that I was called on the 2d of this month, the day after I wrote to you, to visit a patient, the son of one of my own tenants, John Hewson, who was 16 years old on the 26th of February last, and who was in the smallpox, and was at the height on Thursday the 7th. The pustules were large and numerous, though not confluent. This boy was inoculated at Wigton (by Mr. Bell, who is now dead, but who was a very good and attentive surgeon, whom I was well acquainted with, as he was a considerable time under me as surgeon and apothecary to our Dispensary) when he was a month old, which, however, did not succeed. The inoculation was repeated exactly a month after, and at the usual time both arms inflamed, and he was affected with the usual symptoms attending the eruptive fever, afterwards with eruptions, which, though not very numerous, were defined all over his body and limbs, and the pustules were full as long as those he is now affected with, and from which Mr. Bell took matter to inoculate other patients. Thus at the same time we have had two patients in the natural smallpox, one after vaccination, and the other after inoculation.

I will endeavour to procure the burials for the years 1797, 1798, 1799, and 1800, as soon as possible, and will also transmit you the best information in my power respecting queries 1, 2, and 3.—Yours, etc.   J. HEYSHAM.

AN ACCOUNT OF THE BURIALS IN THE PARISHES OF

Years.	St. Mary.	St. Cuthbert.	Wreay Chapelry.	Quakers.†	Total.
1797	176	103	3	2	284
1798	107	85	1	2	195
1799	102	68	1	5	176
1800	180	136	...	2	318
4 years	565	392	5	11	973
1801	134	94	1	7	236
1802	142	101	1	1	245
1803	139	97	1	4	241
1804	170	109	2	6	287
4 years	585	401	5	18	1009
1805	137	68	...	3	208
1806	173	112	5	8	298
1807	191	145	3	6	345
1808	196	116	4	5	321
4 years	697	441	12	22	1172
First 8 years	1150	793	10	29	1982
Second 8 years	1282	842	17	40	2181

[In a future part of the correspondence, apparently, the following memoranda had been sent to Mr. Milne by Dr. Heysham. They will appear appropriately here.—H. L.]

	BURIALS.	Males.	Females.	Total.
1809.	St. Cuthbert	66	93	159
	St. Mary	87	118	205
	Wreay	2	3	5
	Quakers	3	2	5
		158	216	374

* Wreay Chapelry is in the parish of St. Mary, but is separated from it by a portion of St. Cuthbert's intervening. Most of the burials at Wreay are from St. Cuthbert's.

† Only one burial-place for Quakers in the two parishes; it is situated in Fisher Street, St. Mary's, Carlisle.

BURIALS.		Males.	Females.	Total.
1810.	St. Cuthbert	64	63	127
	St. Mary .	81	88	169
	Wreay .	2	1	3
	Quakers .	1	3	4
		148	155	303
1811.	St. Cuthbert .	54	43	97
	St. Mary . .	66	84	150
	Wreay . .	3	3	6
	Quakers . .	4	2	6
		127	132	259
1812.	St. Cuthbert	76	75	151
	St. Mary .	81	101	182
	Wreay .	1	...	1
	Quakers .	2	2	4
		160	178	338
1813.	St. Cuthbert .	105	83	188
	St. Mary . .	79	98	177
	Wreay . .	3	5	8
	Quakers . .	1	3	4
		188	189	377

SUN LIFE OFFICE, 16th April 1814.

DEAR SIR—I received in due course your esteemed favour of the 10th instant, with the valuable documents it enclosed.

Your having separated the burials of the Quakers, and those in the Chapelry of Wreay, from the rest, is highly satisfactory, for it thereby plainly appears that all these have been omitted in the returns to Government ; there must also have been other omissions in the returns, but in some years these are the only deficiencies in the account laid before Parliament.

Your statement of the surveys of 1780 and 1811, distinguishing each of the places mentioned as forming part of the city, suburbs, or villages, is also very valuable to me, and completely satisfies my seventh query, as it furnishes a key to the statements printed by Government, which, with regard to the object of that query, would otherwise have been unintelligible.

Accept my best thanks for your information of the two anomalous cases of natural smallpox, after both the kinds of inoculation ; the subject is extremely curious as well as important.

In expectation of your further information, when it may be perfectly convenient to you, I remain, under the most grateful impressions from your past favours, yours, etc.   JOS. MILNE.

SUN LIFE OFFICE, *20th April* 1814.

DEAR SIR—I was yesterday favoured with yours of the 16th, together with the burials for the four years ending with 1800, and the enumeration in 1801.

It appears singular that, although your numbers always exceed the returns to Government (of the numbers buried) except in the year 1800, for that year they fall 73 short of them—yours being 245, the others 318. It is also worthy of remark, that although the burials in St. Mary's in that year are nearly double what they were in the two preceding years, and about ⅓ as much more than they were in the two following years ; yet those in St. Cuthbert's in 1800 were *less* by about ⅓ than in the preceding or the following years.

I thank you for your useful information respecting the number of prisoners in Carlisle Jail. I had not overlooked them in the Population Abstract for 1801, but purposely omitted them, because I thought it probable they had been omitted in 1811, and because their number is so small, and the persons generally in such periods of life, that, if the jail be well regulated, as I doubt not but that it is (where the magistrates are so intelligent), the mortality in it must be considerably under the general average of the two parishes (including all ages) ; and on these accounts the omission could hardly have had any sensible effect upon the result I was in quest of. But nothing certainly should be neglected that can contribute anything to accuracy ; and now that you have enabled me to do better than guess at the numbers in 1811, I will not fail to include those for 1801.

You add greatly to the value of the documents you favour me with, by the attention you show in transmitting them as quick as you can, that you may delay me the less. It happens, however, that I can make but little use of those

I now have until I obtain the others, which must be combined with them. I therefore wait anxiously, but not impatiently ; and remain, dear Sir, yours, etc.

Jos. Milne.

Carlisle, *April* 24, 1814.

Dear Sir— Queries 1 and 2. The Cumberland Militia consists of 615 rank and file, which have never been stationed in the county since the war. Several of them have wives and families, and a few of the wives and families attend the regiment, but how many is uncertain. A considerable number of Carlisle men have, during the whole course of the war, enlisted in the army and marines, but the exact number cannot be ascertained. We have few or no sailors, scarcely any of the inhabitants having gone into the navy since Mr. Pitt's Navy Quota Act was carried into execution ; and even before that time we procured some of our men from London. I have therefore no hesitation in giving my opinion that 1-30th is by far too great a proportion for our two parishes. You must, however, take into consideration, that as the overseers of the poor took little or no interest in the two surveys of 1801 and 1811, and instead of entering into them with zeal, considered them an additional task imposed on them by Government, there can be no doubt but several omissions took place in both the surveys in the most populous parts of the city and suburbs. The returns from the few villages, I think, we may consider as nearly correct. What, however, was the amount of these omissions will ever remain unknown.

Query 3. Though I consider this query not of much importance, yet it has given me a great deal of trouble. I have made numerous inquiries without having gained any information ; but I have strong reason to believe, from my own recollections, that the survey of 1801 was made either in the month of January or February, or perhaps in both.

When Sir F. Eden published [his work], the workhouse of that part of the parish of St. Mary's which lies within the liberties of the city of Carlisle, and which comprehends Scotch Street, Fisher Street, Castle Street, and Abbey Street, independent of its situation, which is far from good, was, upon the whole, well regulated and conducted. But at that period the workhouse of the parish of St. Cuthbert's and that of Caldew-gate, including Cummersdale, were most miserable receptacles.

The parish of St. Cuthbert has since built one on a healthy elevated situation, about a quarter of a mile from the town, which was finished in 1809, and is well managed. In one of the wings apartments are intended for fever cases, none of which, however, have yet occurred. Within these two years Caldew-gate has taken a new house, and considerable improvement has taken place in the management of it.

	Paupers.
On the 2d of this month St. Cuthbert's contained	48
St. Mary's	31
Caldew-gate	16
	—
	95

This will appear to you a very small number for the population of the place, but considerable sums are paid weekly to paupers in their own houses.

The mortality of the country parishes in the county of Cumberland is certainly considerably less than the mortality of Carlisle. In the years 1780 and 1781 I collected a great deal of information on this subject for the late Mr. Wales of the Charter House, who then had it in contemplation to publish on the population of this island, in answer to Dr. Price's pamphlet on the same subject. If you could possibly procure an inspection of his papers, I am certain they would prove highly interesting and useful.

On an average of ten years, from 1771 to 1780, of a great number of country parishes.

In Leath-ward, one person in 56 and 2-3ds died. In Eskdale-ward one in 54 and ½ died, and the country parishes in Cumberland-ward, as far as my recollection goes, were even more healthy than Leath-ward. See Hutchinson's *History of Cumberland*, vol. i. p. 522.

Independent of the military regularly stationed here since 1809, we have always had, since the commencement of the war, several recruiting parties both for the army and the marines. The constant average number of them, I think, may probably amount to forty or fifty.

I consider it as a most fortunate circumstance that you adverted to the very great difference of the mortality in the two parishes in the year 1800, although, after I received your favour of the 20th, I thought myself almost certain that I was correct ; yet, knowing how liable we all are to error, I immediately re-examined the register of St. Cuthbert's, and to my surprise discovered two leaves of the book adhering, which I must, on my first inspection, have turned over together, and I found the burials for that year, instead of 63, to be 136. Having the book in my possession, I deemed it necessary to re-examine all the four years, and discovered another mistake in 1797 of seven burials, which were entered at the bottom of the page of the burials of 1796, the year being written in pale ink ; therefore, in that year, instead of 96 there were 103 burials.

Burials in both parishes, including [the chapelry of] Wreay and [the] Quakers, in .   .   .   .   1797 were 284

$$
\begin{array}{llr}
\text{in } 1798 & \text{,,} & 195 \\
\text{in } 1799 & \text{,,} & 176 \\
\text{in } 1800 & \text{,,} & 318 \\
\end{array}
$$

Total   973

I think I have now furnished you with all the information in my power, but should you, in the progress of your work, discover any circumstances wanting which I can supply, you may command my services, and you have my full permission to make use of my Observations in the manner you may think proper, taking care to correct any grammatical errors, etc.—I remain, dear Sir, yours, etc.   JOHN HEYSHAM.

P.S.—We have now very few cases of natural smallpox, and only one child has died of that disease since 1st of January.

SUN LIFE OFFICE, 30*th April* 1814.

DEAR SIR—I received on the 27th your esteemed favour of the 24th instant, wherein you have completed the answers to my queries, which have given you so much trouble.   It was not without great reluctance that I troubled you with these last, being well aware that the answers could not add very materially to the mass of valuable information I had previously derived from you.   I had, indeed, made assumptions, which led to almost exactly the same results as the authentic documents you have lately favoured me with, but these *might have been* much wider from the truth : and you have enabled me to give that authenticity to my materials, which removes all ground for doubt or suspicion.

I particularly regret that you should have taken so much trouble to determine in what part of the year 1801 the survey was made.   I did not think it likely that it would be attended with any difficulty, or I should have requested you to take no trouble about it.   The only use I meant to make of it was to determine what the number of the people was on the 1st January 1801, and on the 1st January 1811, as it was in the intervening period that the deaths took place which I was to determine the rate of mortality from ; and it is obvious that, *if the increase of the people was uniform*, the number of the living in the beginning of May in each of those two years would be rather greater than in the beginning of January ; consequently the mean number of the living from the one May to the other would be rather greater than from the one January to the other, which last is that with which the registered burials in the intervening period should be compared.

The late Mr. Wales, master of the mathematical school at Christ's Hospital, did (as well as Mr. Howlett and others) publish a pamphlet on the population of England, in answer to Dr. Price, which I some time ago took great pains to procure, but without success. His books and, I believe, his manuscript papers too, were sold by auction soon after his death, and were, I understood at the time, very productive to his heirs.

I have taken care to make the corrections you were so kind as to direct in your last.

I now see that the autumn will be well advanced before my work will be ready for publication.

I cannot close this letter without acknowledging again the grateful sense I entertain of your polite and kind attentions throughout all the trouble I have given you. Nothing, I am sure, but the most ardent zeal for the promotion of this useful and interesting branch of knowledge, could have carried you through all the drudgery you have undertaken, and executed in the ablest and most satisfactory manner, for, dear Sir, yours, etc. JOS. MILNE.

P.S.—Men of speculative habits, like me, have, you know, but little power of conferring benefits ; but if I can be of any service to you, upon any occasion, I shall be much gratified by your commands, as I should have told you before, had I not expected you to take it for granted.

SUN LIFE OFFICE, 20*th May* 1814.

DEAR SIR—I now beg leave to hand you an estimate of the population and mortality in your two parishes from the commencement of your Observations to the end of last year.

It is not my intention to impose any more tasks upon you. In the Appendix to the work I have in hand I purpose to insert an abstract of your Observations, but (except the information you give respecting the enumeration of 1796) these only extend to the first nine years. It will probably be two or three months or more before that Appendix can be printed, and if, in the meantime, it should

afford you an agreeable amusement at any intervals of leisure, to compare the
variations in the rate of mortality as exhibited in the enclosed Table, at different
times, with the corresponding variations in the circumstances of the people,
especially with regard to the proportion of the wages of labour to the prices of
the necessaries of life, and the presence or absence of epidemical diseases ;
then, by making notes of what might appear to you most worthy of remark,
you would enable me to extend your observations, and would render what is
here attempted much more interesting and instructive.

In constructing the enclosed I have assumed that the population increased
continually and equally in the interval between each of the enumerations of 1780,
1787, 1796, 1801, and until the emigration commenced in 1810 ; 45 are added to
the returned numbers of 1801 and 1811 for the recruiting parties ; 100 for the
regular forces in 1809, 1810, and 1811 ; and 300 in 1812 and 1813. I have considered the population to have increased in 1812, the emigration having then
ceased, and the baptisms having exceeded the burials by 154. The mortality in
1807, you will observe, was considerably greater than in any other of the ten
years from 1801 to 1811, except in 1809 ; and in this last it was so great as
materially to affect the average of the ten.

I should be very sorry if, in consequence of this letter, you took any step that
was irksome to you. If after a short time, when you shall have had leisure to
turn the subject in your mind, you should think it probable that you would ulti-
mately forward me any further observations, I should be obliged by your signi-
fying such expectation to me. The actual mortality since the introduction of
vaccination has not been reduced quite so much in comparison with what it was
from 1779 to 1787, as I should calculate upon from that cause and the decrease
of typhus fever ; probably the operation of some adventitious causes in 1807 and
1809, which you may have it in your power to point out, may account for the
apparent anomaly.—I remain, dear Sir, yours, etc.   JOS. MILNE.

P.S.—The rise or great increase of manufactures in Carlisle, by increasing
the demand for labour, and consequently its recompense, will, I expect, be found
to have had a sensible effect in reducing the rate of mortality ; but I do not
know at what times these took place.

SUN LIFE OFFICE, 23*d March* 1815.

DEAR SIR—I have now the pleasure of transmitting you the work you know
I have been some time engaged upon, and to which you have contributed some
of the most valuable materials.

The expectations of life in Table III. are not exactly the same as those sent you in September 1812, because the Table of Mortality these last were derived from differed a little from the second in the present work, having been deduced only from the deaths in the eight years that intervened between the enumerations in January 1780 and December 1787, and upon the supposition, too, that none died above the age of 100 years.—I remain, yours, etc.   JOS. MILNE.

LONDON, *May* 2, 1815.

MY DEAR SIR—I duly received your kind letter of the 23d April,* and am much gratified by the flattering manner in which you mention my work ; also to learn that so eminent a judge as Dr. Milner [Dean of Carlisle] thinks favourably of it.   If it meet with the reception of the public, which these and the opinions of some other distinguished judges would lead me to hope for, it must be obvious to every reader that it will be owing in a great measure to your own valuable observations.

I beg you to accept of my grateful acknowledgments, both for the services you have rendered in prosecuting the work, and your kind wishes for its success, and remain, dear Sir, yours most faithfully,   JOS. MILNE.

CARLISLE, 14*th June* 1814.

DEAR SIR—I received your favour of the 20th ult., with the enclosed Table of the estimate of the population and mortality of our two parishes, which I have every reason to believe as correct as the subject will admit of.   I think, with very few exceptions, the population has been continually and uniformly increasing since I came to Carlisle until the autumn of 1810.   As, upon research, I can find no memoranda respecting those years in which the mortality was greatest, I dare not venture to suggest any observations from memory.

As you were kind enough, in a former letter, to offer your services, I avail myself of this opportunity to request you will, at your complete leisure, favour me with your opinion on the following subject, which may possibly at some future period prove of advantage to me or my family.   I hold an estate by lease for three lives, of the Corporation of Carlisle, renewable for ever on the payment of a certain fine of twenty shillings on each life, or rather on the renewal of a new life, for I am not bound to renew immediately on the death of the first, or even of the second ; the three lives now being are three of my sons, who are all in perfect health, and have had all the specific epidemic contagious diseases incident to this country, and are of the following ages,—22 years, 21 years, and,

* The copy of Dr. Heysham's letter of the 23d April is lost.

17 years. Query—Should the Corporation be willing to dispose of their interest in this estate to me, what is the exact sum I ought to pay?—Yours, etc.

JOHN HEYSHAM.

LONDON, 22*d June* 1814.

DEAR SIR—In answer to your favour of the 14th inst., I have to inform you that, if you have the lease of an estate dependent on three lives, now aged 22, 21, and 17 years respectively, with the condition that you and your successors may renew it continually whenever any life may fail, by putting in such another as you may think most for your own advantage, upon paying a fine of 20 shillings, then the present value of all the fines that may be paid for such renewals for ever will be 14 shillings and one penny ; upon the supposition that the life renewed with will always be the best that can be found, that is, a healthy one of 7 years of age, the rate of interest being 5 *per cent per annum*, and the law of mortality such as your observations show to have prevailed in Carlisle during the nine years in which they were made. But (the rest being the same) if we use the Northampton Table of Mortality, constructed by Dr. Price, which has generally hitherto been taken for the basis of such calculations, we shall find the value to be one guinea and tenpence halfpenny ($£1 : 1 : 10\frac{1}{2}$). And generally, whatever the fine certain may be, if you multiply it by 704.067, and divide the product by 100.000, the quotient will be the present value of all that may from henceforth be paid for renewals, according to the Carlisle Table. But to obtain the value according to the Northampton Table, this fine must be multiplied by 109.428, and the product divided by 100.000, interest being still reckoned at 5 *per cent.*

I have given the general theorem for the solution of such questions in the 450th article of the work I have in hand, and have shown its application by a numerical example, 645. This is one of the cases wherein the difference in the law of mortality makes a greater difference in the value sought than perhaps any other.

The Expectations of Life, according to the Law of Mortality

At the Age of	Carlisle.	Northampton.	
17	43.57	35.20	According to Dr. Price's Table,
21	40.75	32.90	one person out of 25.18 died
22	40.04	32.39	annually at Northampton.
7	50.80	41.03	

Hence you will see it is of some importance that I should clearly set forth the authority on which the Carlisle Table depends, and show its agreement with the general law of mortality throughout England ; this has been the occasion of most of the trouble I have given you for many months past.   You have enabled me to do it to my own satisfaction, and, may I presume to hope, to the satisfaction of the public.   JOS. MILNE.

To prove to the reader of these pages the great difference between the Carlisle Tables of Mortality, which guided Mr. Milne's reply to Heysham's query, and those of Northampton or some other equally erroneous Tables, which guided the Equitable Assurance Office in 1810, the following reply should be perused. It ought to be stated that Heysham's case, as given above, was put to the Equitable, and here is the reply : " The present value of £1, to be paid on the extinction of each life for ever in the above lease [the lease between the Corporation of Carlisle and Heysham's lives] is two pounds four shillings."
                                        (Signed)   WILLIAM MORGAN.

Equitable Assurance Office, 3d April 1810.

Printed by R. CLARK, *Edinburgh.*